Ari
and the
Barley Queen

ESSENTIAL TRANSLATION SERIES 57

ONTARIO ARTS COUNCIL
CONSEIL DES ARTS DE L'ONTARIO

an Ontario government agency
un organisme du gouvernement de l'Ontario

Canada Council   Conseil des arts
for the Arts   du Canada

Guernica Editions Inc. acknowledges the support of
the Canada Council for the Arts and the Ontario Arts Council.
The Ontario Arts Council is an agency of the Government of Ontario.
We acknowledge the financial support of the Government of Canada
through the National Translation Program for Book Publishing,
an initiative of the *Roadmap for Canada's Official Languages 2013-2018:
Education, Immigration, Communities*, for our translation activities.
We acknowledge the financial support of the Government of Canada.
Nous reconnaissons l'appui financier du gouvernement du Canada.

Pan Bouyoucas

Ari
and the
Barley Queen

Translated by
Sheila Fischman

GUERNICA
EDITIONS
TORONTO • CHICAGO
BUFFALO • LANCASTER (U.K.)
2023

Guernica Founder: Antonio D'Alfonso

Michael Mirolla, editor
Cover and interior design: Rafael Chimicatti
Guernica Editions Inc.
287 Templemead Drive, Hamilton (ON), Canada L8W 2W4
2250 Military Road, Tonawanda, N.Y. 14150-6000 U.S.A.
www.guernicaeditions.com

Distributors:
Independent Publishers Group (IPG)
600 North Pulaski Road, Chicago IL 60624
University of Toronto Press Distribution (UTP)
5201 Dufferin Street, Toronto (ON), Canada M3H 5T8
Gazelle Book Services, White Cross Mills
High Town, Lancaster LA1 4XS U.K.

First edition.
Printed in Canada.

Legal Deposit—Third Quarter
Library of Congress Catalog Card Number: 2022950615
Library and Archives Canada Cataloguing in Publication
Title: Ari and the barley queen / Pan Bouyoucas ;
translated by Sheila Fischman.
Other titles: Ari et la reine de l'orge. English
Names: Bouyoucas, Pan, author. | Fischman, Sheila, translator.
Series: Essential translations series ; 57.
Description: Series statement: Essential translations series ; 57
Translation of: Ari et la reine de l'orge.
Identifiers: Canadiana (print) 20220477612
Canadiana (ebook) 20220477698 | ISBN 9781771838351(softcover)
ISBN 9781771838368 (EPUB)
Classification: LCC PS8553.O89 A8913 2023 | DDC C843/.54—dc23

My dearest daughters,

In the course of my recent travels I heard a story that should interest you – mothers that you now are, and mothers of boys. The woman who related it to me, an emergency room physician of flawless integrity, nevertheless urged me to be discreet when I set it down. That is why I have chosen to turn it into a tale, a genre that lends itself well to preserving anonymity, of both people and places. I have not however converted the malicious mother into a stepmother. If one did so in times past, to protect the persona of the loving and devoted mother, women writing today would laugh at such a subterfuge, all the more so as many of them have placed the hidden truth of their birth mother at the core of their work. Strangely, their male counterparts avoid the subject, at least in our part of the world. They are not averse, however, to skewering the overbearing father. Why not the possessive mother, then, jealous and devouring? Psychologists would be better qualified than I to answer that question. I am but a teller of tales, and the most I can hope for is that the story I'm about to relate might spare my grandsons some of the excesses of maternal love.

1

THE KING AND QUEEN OF BARLEY had two sons. The eldest was blessed with great beauty and with virtues that matched his outward appearance, and his mother had named him Ari, which in the local dialect meant flawless, exceptional. But nature is sometimes wanton in her endowments. The younger, who was neither ugly nor stupid, had been dealt a grievous stutter. The barley queen called him Junior, and laughed when he said he l-l-l-loved her dearly and that he would m-m-m-marry her when he was g-g-g-grown-up. Junior assumed that he was his mama's favourite because when her older son told her the same thing, she didn't laugh and her eyes filled with water.

Then the two brothers grew as two boys do, and the girls of their age came to play a larger role in their dreams than their mother.

Even if her elder son became distant, the barley queen was proud of the admiration he inspired. Until the day when he invited one of his female admirers to the castle. And what a castle! The barley business was so productive that the queen had been able to create the replica of an English manor house whose majesty contrasted sharply with the nearby farms and cottages.

If the barley king's welcome to his son's girlfriend was warm, the barley queen's was borderline polite. With her hair pulled up in a bun on her head like a crown and wearing a designer dress that local girls could only dream of, she said to her eldest:

"Give your friend a tour of the castle. It's probably the only time she'll be able to see such an interior."

High on her highest heels, she added, for the enlightenment of the guest:

"Ari will inherit it once he finds a girl of his own class. A lion cannot marry a goat, is that not so?"

When the girl left, the queen spoke only of her faults. The same for the second, the third, and the fourth. One was too fat, another too thin, this one too talkative, that one too constipated. In short, no female friend of the prince found favour in her eyes. And when the barley king told her that every individual arrived on earth with his or her own portion of beauty, you just had to ferret it out, his wife instantly imposed her own point of view, which amounted to the same unanswerable judgment, as cutting as the tone of her voice: her son, inheritor of the barley kingdom, merited nothing but the best.

Ari was unaware of his girlfriends' failings until his mother brought them to light. At times her remarks weakened his interest. At other times he found them so unfair that his feelings for the young woman were only enhanced. His mother would then call up the girl's parents. As most of the region's inhabitants worked for her, the queen threatened to fire them if their offspring did not remove themselves from her heir's life.

Furious, Ari asked his father to intervene. But the barley king dared not contradict his wife's orders.

"Be patient, my boy," he said to his son. "What you feel for girls at your age is purely carnal. And carnality clouds one's judgment. As a woman, your mother sees beyond the physical charms that stir up boys' hormones and passions, and she'll be able to find you an appropriate companion."

Ari had seen enough of girls to arouse his interest, but too little to summon up his patience. However, the girls at his college no longer dared to approach him. There were others, of course, but Ari was timid with the ones he didn't know, and so unaware of his power of seduction that, when he was stared at, he thought he was being taken for someone else, or that something was hanging off the end of his nose.

Desperate, he appealed to his maternal grandmother. She was the only person the barley queen was not able to control. She dearly loved her grandson, and above all, she was well versed in the art of magic spells.

In fact, when Ari told her about his dilemma, his granny handed him a little bag containing the dried blood of a rooster, and told him to deposit three pinches of it under his pillow while making a wish. When he will have slept over it for one whole night, the next day his wish would be granted.

Back in the castle, Ari placed three pinches of dried rooster blood under his pillow while praying that he would quickly find a girl to his taste and also to that of his mother. And the next morning, he knew that the spell had succeeded when the barley queen, in order to contain the hormonal urges of her elder son, informed him that from now on he would be spending his free time with her in order that he might familiarize himself with the culture and commerce of barley.

Ari had no interest whatsoever in the agricultural exploits of his parents – he had a passion for History and worshiped the great men who had marked it – but he knew that many girls worked in barley production. So he would go there after school and, when he found the one he was looking for, he would make her pregnant before introducing her to his mother, who would have no choice but to bless their union. There would perhaps be no extravagant wedding, no great jubilation or fireworks, perhaps not even a banquet, but one thing was certain: He and his beloved would be able to love each other to their hearts' content and live happily ever after.

2

ARI DREAMED ALL MORNING about this coupling. But when he arrived after school at his parents' place of business, he didn't find a single girl whose body and soul he would want to unite with his own. His mother had replaced all the young workers with women who were older or married. However, she had kept on her desk the portrait of her oldest offspring, side by side in a double frame with a photo of her pregnant self, on which was scrawled in a child's handwriting: *This is me Ari when I was in mama's heart.*

Ari went back to see his grandmother and told her:

"A spell has been cast on me, granny. I want to be a man and my mother thinks I'm still five years old."

His granny sat him down at the table where she used to place him when she told him, as he drank her chocolate, stories about the time when she was his age. Stories that always ended happily, because they followed the old adage that every cloud has a silver lining. But his grandmother didn't tell Ari any stories now, nor did she serve him chocolate. She did put a bowl on the table, but she filled it with water. She let fall a drop of oil into the water and then, performing a series of movements that made her bracelets clink, she pronounced a few incomprehensible words for her grandson, and the drop of oil broke in two.

"You're right," the old lady declared. "Someone has given you the evil eye."

Ari thought about his brother. Because of his stutter, he had no success with girls, and whenever Ari brought one to the castle, Junior eyed her as if he were casting a spell. Fortunately, his granny had seen all this, and would be freeing him.

Which is what she did, ordering her beloved grandson to spit three times into the bowl, then to pour its contents into the toilet and flush it all down.

The next day, when he went to the barley kingdom after school, Ari found the same women, and he was wondering whether his granny had lost her gift, when an employee suddenly fell ill. As all the workers were busy and as no one had yet assigned him a task, Ari offered to take the sick worker home. An offer that changed his life after meeting at the sick worker's house her young daughter.

Her name was Moli and she was as beautiful as Ari was handsome. But while Ari was not aware of his beauty – which made him all the more seductive – Moli was fully aware of her charms, and was much less timid. She thanked Ari for having accompanied her mother, and then, after having taken a good look at him, asked him if he would go with her to the cemetery after nightfall.

"Why to the cemetery, at night?" Ari asked.

Moli explained that she adored the theatre, and hoped to enter the Conservatory in the capital. But first she had to take an audition and to pass it. She had already chosen her text, but she had no one to feed her her lines. The boys she knew could hardly read or talked through their noses, which made her laugh, even though the scene was tragic. And so, she fell back on sighs and sustained sounds.

"What's sustained sounds?"

Moli stood Ari in front of a mirror. Then, with the tips of her breasts brushing against the boy's back, she said to him:

"Make little sighs thinking about all the lying that goes on in politics, about terrorism and greenhouse gases. Now make them stronger, like a mourner wailing in a fit of lamentation. Have you noticed? With every breath, your body leans backwards, while the sound you emit tends to bend forwards."

"Is that all it takes to play your role?"

"That just helps with my posture. The emotion in the lines can only be absorbed through the body. And to help my body feel the character's pain, I rehearse in the cemetery at night, when no one is there."

Ari felt the pressure of Moli's breasts on his back for the rest of the day. When he finally got home, he washed and spruced himself up. Then, leaving his cell phone behind so that no-one's voice could possibly intrude, he went out at nightfall, through his bedroom window, and didn't stop running until he came to the cemetery gate.

3

♦

Moli was waiting with two copies of her script and two bottles of water. She'd also brought two lanterns on chains. One, she hung around Ari's neck, the other, around her own. To illuminate the text, she explained, lighting them. Flashlights would have worked better, but the lanterns were more appropriate to the ancient scene they were about to rehearse and to the setting in which they found themselves.

Moli then talked about the two characters in the scene, the conflict that threatened the couple, how she was calling upon her sensory memory in order to interiorize the heroine she wanted to become. To help Ari feel the passion that bound his character to hers, she also gave him a kiss that forever branded her on his lips and soul, warning him all the while that she wouldn't let him touch her further. Not before the end of the rehearsal, for sure. Explaining that even after a simple kiss, it took her an eternity just to find her voice.

"Don't be afraid of ridicule," she said. "Even professional actors have trouble expressing emotion at first readings."

They rehearsed every night that weekend, and every night the following week. And the more Moli transformed into her character, the more the glow from her lantern seemed to shine out from herself, transforming all her being into an ethereal creature.

When they finally stopped, bathed in sweat and exhausted, they doused the lanterns, swallowed what water was left in their bottles, then abandoned themselves to the passion now alive in their bodies swathed in shadow. But if Moli embraced Ari with as much ardor as he put into his kisses, she refused to remove her underpants. In compensation, she would administer what she called a "perk" to the part of Ari's body that their caresses had enlarged. They would then go home, Moli reviewing the rehearsal, and Ari thinking about how he would get her to take off her panties, convinced at his age that after making her pregnant, the path of their lives would be as smooth as the skin of his beloved.

Perhaps, he said to himself one night, I would succeed if, instead of emptying a bottle of water, we were to drink wine after the rehearsal.

The next day, he descended, on the sly, into the castle cellar and made off with one of the best bottles. But when, trembling with impatience, he reached the cemetery, Moli was not there.

He waited for an hour, watching the stars travel across the sky, in order to distract himself from the dead bodies surrounding him, then he went to ring at her door.

"She's gone," Moli's mother told him. "She left you a letter. Read it and you'll understand."

My darling love,

I told a friend that I was rehearsing my text with you, my friend told others, your mother learned about it, and she threatened to fire my mother if I did not leave the kingdom.

When you read this note, I will already be on the train. There is no point asking my mother where I am going, she had to swear not to tell a soul.

Oh, Ari, it's so hard to believe that we'll never see one another again. We've only known each other for ten nights, but I'll remember every one of them for all my life. And when I leave this vale of tears, I want to be buried in our cemetery, since you will be there too.

Swear to me that you will not forget that I loved you. That as bridegroom and king, you will remember my sustained sounds, my lanterns, and my perks.

May the heavens be with you, my love,

Your Moli

4

ARI DID NOT, AS he'd done on other nights, enter through his bedroom window. He went in by the main door, confronted his mother, who was preparing for bed, and said:

"In all the photographs of me that you've saved – on your dressing table, in your study – I'm no more than ten years old. Wake up. I'm no longer ten years old."

Her hair undone, face stripped of cosmetics and colours, voice quavering, his mother begged him to speak more quietly.

"I have a fever," she said. "We'll talk tomorrow."

Was she really sick, or was this a delaying tactic?

"I won't be here tomorrow."

The barley queen did not lose her temper. Calmly addressing her son as though he were a child, she told him that one day he would thank her for what she'd done, that every "exchange of saliva" with Moli had been calculated, that she only wanted to become pregnant in order to fleece him, and that he deserved better. The daughter of the beer king, perhaps. With her brewery and her respect for barley, she would turn their two kingdoms into a financial empire and make her husband the richest and most powerful man in the land.

"Introduce her to Junior," Ari replied.

Certain that Moli had gone to the capital to take her audition at the Conservatory, he added:

"I have other plans. I'm going to the capital to study history."

As we know, the barley queen couldn't bear any contradiction, and became furious at the slightest sign of opposition. But this was a very delicate situation, and her dream of becoming the mother of the richest and most powerful man in the land was at stake. The brewer's daughter on whom she'd set her sights would never marry a boy who took a whole minute to say hello. But she also knew that at the age, the true age, of her older son, one is prepared, for the slightest infatuation, to imperil one's entire life. Rather than continuing to rail against the woman who was seeking her crown in the heart of her prince, she came out with a loud lament, followed by a sentence that in circumstances such as this one, flies to the rescue of mothers:

"I wish you a child that will cause you as much pain as you're causing me right now!"

The croaking had disappeared from her voice.

"So many disappointments, such bitterness! Lord, what have I done to deserve them? I have let a thousand opportunities escape me and as many dreams disappear, in order to bear and to bring up the future barley king. And what have I harvested? Scorn, lies, tears of blood. I, who was so happy when he agreed to learn the craft. Hallelujah, I said to myself, the succession is assured. I will be able to see Venice, visit the Taj Mahal, shop on the Champs Élysées. While he thought of nothing but to scratch at his juvenile itches. And once he got a taste of other nipples, he forgot the ones that had fed him. Why, my angel, this aversion for the woman who loves you the most in the world? I built this castle for you and your descendants. I even offer you the chance to make your mark, like the great men you admire. Don't study history, make it."

Ari could well repeat and swear that he loved her and was grateful for everything she'd done for him, when she did not obtain all the concessions she demanded, his mother's tears flowed more abundantly, attracting the attention of her husband and younger son.

"It's all your fault," she said to the barley king as he entered her room.

"Excuse me?"

"If you had let me deliver a few slaps like my sister did, we wouldn't be here. She's always been luckier than me. A husband who supports her unconditionally. And a son – she only has one, but what a son. Not chasing after whores, always with his mother, listening to her and honouring her as he should."

"Allow me to remind you," her husband said, "that your nephew does not chase after whores because he lost the use of his legs after a motorcycle accident, and is glued to a wheelchair, and depends on his mother for all his needs. Is that the ideal son you would have wished for?"

19

Caught, the barley queen wavered, then sank onto her bed, saying that she was dying. Ari, who was used to such excesses, left the room, while his father, all contrite, waved a fan over his wife's face, shouting to Junior to bring her a glass of water.

Ari hardly had time to reach his room before his mother's groans turned again to a roar.

"You too, you want to see him ruined?" she said to her husband. "Let his whore pay for his history lessons! You will not give him a cent! And I warn you, if that Judas and his slut set foot in this castle, it will be over my dead body!"

5

T HE NEXT DAY, Ari went to see his grandmother
and said:

"Why is my mother so hard on me? I'm her child,
she ought to want me to be happy."

"Dear heart, you do not marry the first girl who
catches your eye."

"I don't love her for her beauty, granny. She has
something special. I can't describe it in words, but
when I'm with her, I'm filled with joy. Even when
she's not there, just her name carries me away, simply
saying it."

"Say it then, and fly to her."

"My mother will never open her door to her. She
said so. Never again will I set foot in the castle with
Moli unless it's over her dead body. Help me to change
her mind."

"You might as well try to reroute the lines that criss-
cross the palms of her hands. Your mother will only
open her door to a girl she'll have chosen for you. A
girl who's filthy rich. A girl you won't love more than

you love your mother. Above all, a daughter-in-law she can control as she controls everyone else."

"She doesn't control me and she never will."

"Then go and find your sweetheart."

"I don't know where she is. Probably in the capital. But the capital is big. Help me to locate her."

The old lady gave him her blessing. Ari wanted more but, repeating that he had to find Moli quickly because he needed her the way he needed air to breathe, he encountered only refusals. And rebukes.

"Listen to me carefully," his grandmother said in a tone of voice she'd never used with him. "You want the ball? No amulet, prayer, or incantation will make it come to you."

"And the blood of the rooster? The drop of oil?"

"Fairy-tale notions to comfort ninnies and cowards and to bolster their illusions. If you don't want to spend your life bemoaning your fate, get this into your head: You have to chase after the ball to get the ball. So do you want my blessing or not?"

Ari left, slamming the door, persuaded that his most faithful ally, the only person to whom he'd confided his most cherished secrets and hopes, had only reeled out this nonsense so as not to incur, by helping him, the rage of the barley queen.

He didn't even have enough money to buy a train ticket for the capital, and had no one to ask for it. And so he decided to punish his mother and his grandmother by putting an end to his life, and neither the glances shot his way from the girls he met nor their smiles could deter him from his baleful plan.

He found a rope, then went to the cemetery to hang himself on the site of his bygone happiness.

There were still people and he waited for night, rereading Moli's farewell note and recalling in his thoughts, haloed by lantern light, the magical moments he'd shared with her. Keep moving, train, he said when he heard it whistling in the distance. Go and tell the one I love that her prince has been condemned to die well before his time because he refused to become the carbon copy of his mother's expectations. Tell her that he will await her, as agreed, at our memories' graveyard, when her life in turn will have ended.

Having thus shed the tears that remained to him, at nightfall he set himself to preparing a hangman's noose.

No sooner had he finished than he heard moaning.

Was there still someone in the cemetery?

He approached the source of the noise to check, and made out in the shadows a silhouette that iced his blood.

Sitting at the edge of a grave, a young man raised a stout staff with both hands and, as if it were a hammer, brought it down heavily onto his legs, then let it drop and pressed his hands to his mouth, as if to prevent the emergence of a cry.

Ari thought it was a corpse escaped from its earthen bed. He only recovered from his fright when, striking his legs once more with his rod, the fellow let out a curse.

"D-d-dammit t-t-to hell!"

"What are you doing there?" Ari cried, throwing himself on his brother to pull away the staff.

Now it was Junior's turn to think he'd seen a ghost. And when he'd recovered from his fright, he said to his older brother:

"I c-c-can't t-t-take it anymore. F-f-father crying, thinking you've g-g-gone. M-m-mother on the telephone with the b-b-beer king, talking about your m-m-marriage to his little girl. M-m-maybe by c-c-crippling myself like our c-c-cousin, she'll stop sneering at m-m-me like I was a p-p-piece of dirt and p-p-pay attention to me."

Despite his stammer, his tears, and his runny nose, he inspired only respect in the eyes of his elder. All things told, Junior was showing more courage than he had in pursuing his most cherished desire. So Ari said to him:

"Go back to the castle. You will be the only son, the only heir. I am leaving the kingdom and never coming back. Go. Tell them that you hurt your legs while trying to hold me back. They will have to admire you."

6

Aᴿᴵ ʀᴇᴛᴜʀɴᴇᴅ to his grandmother to ask for her forgiveness and her blessing. She gave them to him, along with some money, and he was able to take the night train.

As soon as he was seated, he switched on the light in order to study the street map of the capital that he'd picked up at the station. But a plump little man dressed to the nines, sitting in the same row on the other side of the aisle, stared at him and let out a grunt. Thinking that his light was interfering with his neighbour's sleep, Ari switched it off and watched the landscape flow by.

The sky was cloudless, a full moon lit up the sea of barley as the train passed through it, but Ari saw only Moli.

"You can't shut your eyes either?" the neighbour said. "You have worries?"

"On the contrary, I'm going to join my sweetheart."

The neighbour grunted again.

"You ought to be all smiles. In fact, a good-looking young man like you ought to always have a smile on his lips."

Ari deduced from the man's words and the way he delivered them that he was one of those not at all indifferent to the attractions of a beautiful boy. Under other circumstances, he would have cut short the exchange right there. But the man spoke like a resident of the capital, and the map he had bought only featured museums, large monuments, the train station, and a few governmental buildings. He would save a lot of time if the fellow could show him the location of the Conservatory and the hotels and lodgings where a student of limited means could stay.

"You couldn't have come to a better person," the man replied. "I work just across from the Conservatory, and I know the area well."

He sat down with Ari and showed him on the map the location of the Conservatory, of a few hotels and boarding houses, as well as that of the department store he managed.

"If you plan to stay in the capital and are looking for work," he said, "I would be pleased to count you among our employees."

He gave Ari his card, grunting once more when their fingers touched.

"If you don't mind my asking," Ari asked, "why do you grunt?"

"To chase away certain thoughts. When I experience a sudden urge, a dark idea, or remorse, to rid myself of it …"

"You make those noises."

"Usually one is enough. Sometimes I need two, or three. Especially at night when dreams and youthful idiocies turn into adult nightmares. During the day, work blocks them out. At night, drink and television obscure them as I await the deliverance of sleep. Alas, even that final refuge is becoming more and more precarious. Why, last night, I had barely gone to bed, when I remembered the time I pushed away my father when he came to greet me at the station on my return from summer camp. Why did I think of that all of a sudden? I was thirteen years old, and at the age of thirteen it's embarrassing for a boy to be kissed by his father in front of his friends. Never again did my dad take me in his arms. If he were still alive, I would throw myself at him to embrace him. But he's gone. Just like the childhood friend I lost by treating him like dirt one night because he couldn't jump in the air as high as me. Since then I've had dozens of friends, I rarely think about them, while he comes back to haunt me every time I see the moon. I've consulted a psychiatrist. A professional consoler, too, who prides himself on being able to calm any psychic suffering just through the use of words. I even tried contempla-tion. They say that the contemplation of nature helps us to free ourselves from remorse and to make peace with the past. Me, I caught pneumonia … Ah! if only I could run into him one day. I would throw myself at his feet. I'm vermin, I would tell him, the lowest of the low! Allow me, so I may redeem myself, to lick your boots with my cruel and perfidious tongue!"

Carried away by his confession, he had placed his pudgy hand over that of Ari.

"Why do you remember him when you see the moon?" Ari asked, quietly removing his hand in order to fold up the map of the capital.

"When I treated him like dirt, we were jumping in the air, our arms raised, in order to catch it."

"I did the same thing when I was little. I jumped in the air to grab the moon when it was full."

"What extraordinary coincidences," the man said. "The same train, the same row, the same destination, the same desire to catch the moon. It's surely a sign. I believe very much in signs."

His hand once more grasped Ari's.

"I'm going to help you find your loved one," he said. "You'll stay with me and we'll tour together the hotels and boarding houses. If we don't find her there, I'll speak to the teachers and employees at the Conservatory. They all come to buy their provisions at my establishment. The students as well. One of them is bound to tell us where she is staying."

Ari thanked him, and wondered how he could free his hand this time without insulting him, when suddenly the train slowed, and all the lights came on. Thinking they were entering a station, Ari looked outside and saw his father's private helicopter landing between the rail line and the forest that ran along beside it.

"I beg you," he said to the man as he was leaving his seat, "don't tell them you've seen me."

7

As soon as his feet touched the ground, he ran to hide behind a tree, and waited to climb back on the train until his father and the two policemen who had come with him had finished their search. But when the three men got off, they stayed near the rails until the train left, to make sure that he didn't get back on. And after the train melted into the night and silence returned, the barley king called to his son and begged him to leave his hiding place and come back to the castle with him.

"This forest is a labyrinth," he said. "You'll die in there. Your mother and I are only thinking about what's best for you, and every day we thank the Lord for having given us a son who's so brilliant that he will know how to preserve and expand what we'll have left him as an inheritance. Give us at least a month for all the hopes we've invested in you. At the end of a month if you still want to leave, I'll take you to the capital myself, by helicopter. You believe me, don't you? Why don't you answer me? At least tell me that you hear me. How can I go back home knowing that my son is lost in this forest?"

The very mention of his mother and the fate she had in store for him was enough to drive Ari away. But he could not tear his eyes from the silhouette of his old man which he could clearly pick out under the full moon. *What should I do, granny?* he pondered. *If I move away, he'll spend the night here looking for me, and I will spend the rest of my life grunting like the man on the train, chasing the memory of this voice that is rending my heart. If I show up to embrace him and tell him that it's not his word I doubt, but the intentions of his wife, the policemen will jump me, as they'd been ordered to do, to bring me back, consenting or by force. Tell me what to do.*

Of course, his grandmother couldn't fly to his aid like the genies and the goddesses who inhabited the tales she told him. It was one of the policemen, who, unknowing, came to his rescue when, taking pity on the barley king, said to him:

"He probably stayed on the train. We looked in every car, but not on the roof. We didn't think of looking there."

The barley king then asked him to call the police in the capital to make them search the train's roof when it pulled into the station. Meanwhile, he added, they ought to take a look behind some trees. Just in case.

The policeman pulled out his cell phone to call his colleagues in the capital, while his partner and the barley king directed flashlight beams toward the trees behind which Ari was hiding. This forced him to move deeper into the forest, promising himself to call his father as soon as he got his hands on a phone.

The farther he went, the denser the forest became, and the less light was cast by the moon. Soon he was groping his way, bumping into a trunk, tripping over a stump or a root, grazing his hands on bark and thorns, a branch slashing at his face every three or four steps. Still, he didn't stop until his legs could no longer hold him up. He sat on the ground to rest and await the day, blaming his mother all the more. If she had not sent his father to look for him, he would have soon arrived at the capital. But his father had once again given in to his wife's demands. How not to blame him too, a little?

Ari began walking again at dawn, now calling on his grandmother to guide his steps toward a village, or toward a road, at least.

A few hours later, still seeing nothing but trees all around him, he was thinking that he'd never emerge from this wooded labyrinth when he came to a clearing in the middle of which rose a tree the likes of which he had never seen, even as a child, when he was still of an age when all things appeared larger than they really were.

8

THE TREE had the circumference of a lighthouse, and was just as tall. Equally impressive was the cabin built in its branches, three metres from the ground, accessible by a rope ladder.

"Is anyone there?" Ari asked.

A man emerged from the trees at the other end of the clearing. Tall, thin, and bent, wearing a beekeeper's suit with a veil that masked his face.

"Sir," Ari said, "I am lost, and I am dying from hunger and thirst."

"Feed yourself from the forest," the man replied. "What's in the clearing is mine and mine alone."

"I have money, I'll pay you."

"I care about your money as much as my bees care for your shoes. Go on your way."

"At least tell me what direction I must take to reach a village or the road."

"You've come into the forest without water and without a compass? That's not very smart, young man."

Ari replied that he had not entered the forest by choice, and then he told his story, talked about the barley kingdom, his passion for Moli, and his mother's cruelty in exiling her just as he was preparing to make her pregnant. All he wanted was to be reunited with his beloved, he said. But he was plagued by misfortune, otherwise he would be with his beloved at this moment.

Touched by his story, the man promised to guide him to the road where he would certainly find someone to take him to the capital, or at least to the next village. But the light of day was dimming in the leaves, and as he would have to walk several kilometres, he invited Ari to spend the night with him.

In the cabin, he took off his beekeeper's suit, revealing a gaunt face as old as the forest, with eyes that were beginning to cloud. As far as his meagre means allowed, he served Ari food and drink. Ari thanked him for his hospitality, then asked the man if he had a telephone.

"Those who have something more beautiful and more intelligent to tell me than silence may all be found there," the old man replied, pointing to a shelf of books.

"My poor father," Ari said, sighing. "He must be desperate now that he knows that I wasn't on the roof of the train."

To take his mind off his troubles, the old hermit told him about a girl he'd wanted to impregnate by making her drunk not with wine, but with high-flown language and ideas.

"Television was her culture though and the source of her dreams," he said, "and she left me after two months for a stand-up comedian. And as she laughed at the idiocies of that clown, I shed tears so abundantly that clouds formed over my head. If you don't want to suffer the same fate, be careful not to use the strategy of wine, my boy. All women want a child. Like flowers, their attractions have no other goal but to attract the bees we are and to perpetuate the species. But if the expedient of philosophy bores them, that of wine only inspires indignation and scorn. To make your Moli pregnant, get her drunk with laughter. When a woman laughs she is disarmed, you can do with her what you want."

"My grandmother was right to say that every cloud has a silver lining," Ari said. "If my father had not stopped the train, I would never have known that wine would make me lose the love of my life. What strategy would you recommend to free me from the picture of my father? On the train, I met a man who banished his feelings of remorse by emitting groans."

"Groans will only dispel remorse for a moment or two. To get free of it forever …"

"Yes, please tell me."

The hermit brought out of a box a long skirt, flowered and perfumed, and told Ari to put it on if he wanted to know how to shield himself from remorse.

Ari thought of the man in the train, and replied:

"Not on your life!"

"That's human gratitude for you," the hermit said. "I give him shelter. I impart to him the honey of a life. I even promise to lead him to the road though

34

I can hardly stand on my feet. And he shows me as much respect as the animals that eat my vegetables."

Ari's fear of remaining a prisoner of the forest and never seeing Moli again made him quickly change his tone.

"Sir," he said, "I want to express my thanks to you. Without your help. I would have lost not only Moli, but my life as well. I only ask you to tell me why you want to have me wear a skirt."

9

♦

His books, his bees, and his vegetable garden were enough to distract him from his solitude. When, every two or three years, someone passed by, he exchanged a few sentences and saw them on their way, wanting only to be left alone with his silence and contemplation. Ari was the first person he'd invited to climb up with him, and probably the last, ripe as he was for the maggots to take over his body. Still, before being feasted upon, he wanted one more time to experience the pleasure of an affectionate hand playing in his hair.

"That's all I ask. To rest my head on your lap for an hour, and to inhale the perfume of this skirt while you stroke my head, without saying a word. You don't even have to take off your pants, just slide the skirt over them. After, I'll tell you how to shield yourself from remorse for all time."

Ari slipped the skirt over his pants.

The old man took a small flask and emptied its contents into his mouth. To help him forget that Ari was a man, he explained to his young guest, then said:

"Did I tell you that my tree is the tallest in the forest? From its top, you can see for kilometres all around. I haven't made my way up for at least ten years. Don't have the strength. And my eyes are so dim that I can't even read."

Ari stroked his head. And remembered when his mother used to play in his hair. He would experience such sybaritic charms then that he found all sorts of pretexts for laying his head in her lap. Adding, to arrive at his goal, that in return for her caresses, he would take her around the world when he was grown.

I hope the hermit will also know how to make me forget this promise, he said to himself.

However, his caresses put the old man to sleep, and, not having the heart to wake him, he too nodded off, and only woke when he heard dogs barking.

Not having found him on the roof of the train, his father had obviously ordered a hunt.

The hermit's head still rested in his lap. Ari shook him so he would lead him to the road, but he didn't stir.

Ari had never touched a corpse, and the very idea of having spent the night with a dead man's head in his lap shook him to the point of nausea.

What rotten luck! he said. *He survived for more than eighty years. Why did he have to croak now?*

Then he remembered the flask the hermit had emptied into his mouth. Doubtless it contained a poison. Why else would he have said that his tree was the highest in the forest, and that he'd be able to see for kilometres all around from its top. He knew that he would not be waking to lead him to the road.

But then, why had he promised to tell him how to free himself from his remorse? And above all, why had he chosen to die on this night?

Ari was still wondering about this when he again heard the dogs. He took off the skirt and climbed to the top of the tree, from where he could indeed see for kilometres all around, in particular the highway that crossed the land from north to south, on the east. How to reach it before the dogs tracked him down? They had picked up his scent and their barks were coming near.

Help me, granny, I can't fly off this tree like a bee.

As he said that last word, his face lit up, and he descended so fast that he scraped his hands and legs.

Back in the cabin, he pulled on the old man's suit and gloves, then climbed down the ladder back to earth.

The voices and the barking were now very near. And when the dogs and the police burst into the clearing, Ari raised the lid on one hive, tossed it in their direction, then took off toward the east, while the yapping behind him turned into howls and the voices into curses, accompanied by a concert of slaps the pursuers were applying to their faces, necks, and arms.

Ari didn't stop running until he came to the highway. He took off the suit – he'd disposed of the gloves along the way – and having no more veil, was dazzled by the sun that was flaring over the world and missed a gradient; a sharp pain shot through his right leg, and he collapsed full length at the feet of a woman whose white dress was a radiant glimmer against the sky.

10

S HE WAS AN EMERGENCY room doctor, whose hat had blown off when she was at the wheel of her convertible, and she had stopped to retrieve it. She helped Ari, whose ankle had instantly swollen up, to her car, settled him in the back seat so that he could stretch out his leg, then got back on the road and asked him what he was doing in the middle of nowhere.

Ari told her his story. And when they arrived at the small town where the woman lived and had her practice, he asked her to leave him at the bus station so he could catch the next one leaving for the capital.

The ER doctor instead took him to the hospital so his foot could be x-rayed.

"It's only dislocated," she said, after examining the film. "You'll be walking again in two weeks."

"Why two weeks?" Ari asked. "If there's no fracture …"

"Even if there's no fracture, your injury requires you to rest the joint until you're cured, otherwise there will be consequences. Instead of complaining, be glad that you happened to fall at my feet. I'm a doctor, I have a guest room with a private bath, and I can treat your ankle as required. Your cheeks, your hands, and your legs as well. They're all scratched up."

Which is what she did. After having bandaged Ari's ankle to stabilize it, she disinfected his scratches, found him some crutches, then drove him to her home, asking him to lower his head so the neighbours wouldn't see him. Their mask of virtue, she said, had 36 eyes as viperish as their tongues, and they would natter away to their hearts' delight if they saw her in the company of a stranger, especially one who was half her age. And so Ari lowered his head and only raised it when the doctor had parked her car in her garage. She then showed him the guest room and advised him not to open the curtains. The window gave onto the street and he could be seen.

"Instead, open the French window. It opens onto the garden, like my bedroom. And my garden is surrounded by a high wall, because I like to sunbathe in the nude."

Ari thanked her for all the help she'd given him, and was continuing to give, then asked if he could use her telephone.

He wanted to contact his father so he wouldn't be worried about him. To avoid being assailed with his grievances once again, he composed his secretary's number, taking care to hide the number of the caller, and asked her to tell her employer that he was in the capital and that he was fine.

He then found and composed the number of the Conservatory. If Moli were registered for the auditions, they would have her phone number, and he could call her to tell her that he had not forgotten her, that he'd be in the capital in two weeks at the most.

But the information concerning the students was confidential. They wouldn't even say whether Moli was scheduled for the auditions.

"Let me deal with it," the ER doctor said. "My brother lives in the capital, and he's a deputy. As a politician, he makes a point of knowing everyone who might one day help his career. The director of the Conservatory is certainly on his list, and he will know how to obtain the information you need. Meanwhile, you should have a bath. After two days in the forest, you need it badly. Then take a pill for your pain, and sleep for a while."

Five minutes later, when she came to collect his clothes in order to wash them, she saw him naked in the bathtub. "God, it's good to look at a beautiful man!" she exclaimed, even if it took a lot to impress a woman of her experience. Ari hid his nakedness, astonished that a doctor almost as old as his mother could say such a thing. *She must have been joking*, he said to himself. Then sought in the bathroom mirror the object of her sarcasm.

11

WHEN HE WAKENED from his nap, Ari went to find the ER doctor to ask if she had spoken to her brother, and he found her in the garden. She was wearing only her hat and sandals, and a dozen multi-coloured parakeets were flitting around her. "Make me a coffee," one cried. "Shut your trap, bitch," said another. "Open your legs," said a third.

"Every time I'm tempted to live with someone," the woman said to Ari as she slipped on a robe, "I buy a parakeet and teach it one of the expressions spouses are known for."

"You're fat," piped up a bird.

"Okay, that's enough," the doctor said.

She opened the door of the cage, and when all the birds were inside, she covered it with a sheet to silence them. She then settled Ari on two chairs, and as she served him food and drink, she told him that her brother had not been able to locate Moli, because the registration for the Conservatory auditions would only take place in two and a half weeks.

Ari had been so eager to tell his beloved that they would soon be together again that this news put him in an even worse mood. However much the ER doctor tried to change the subject, he kept harping on the same tune, now cursing the egotistical ferocity of his mother and the cowardice of his father, now talking about Moli, whose remoteness had multiplied her charms and the strength of the love that bound them. If he'd had a thousand photos of her, he would have shown them all to the ER doctor. But he only had the note his beloved had left him, and he kept it on his person like a sacred relic. He read it to the ER doctor twice, and would have done so a third time had the wine not blurred his vision. Fearing that his hostess would notice his drunkenness, and laugh at his desire to take possession of a woman when he was intoxicated after two glasses, he pretended that his ankle was throbbing and that he ought to retire. The doctor led him to his room, laid him out on the bed, and massaged his foot and then his whole leg. She did this with such expertise that, despite his sorrow and his desire to make Moli the only woman in his life, Ari could not stop his body from paying homage to the ER doctor's fingers and the well-being they procured him.

"Does my prince like that?" she asked. "Is he happy at last?"

Ari wanted to conceal the outward manifestation of his appreciation, but the woman had taken notice, and he could not see her so moved by it without being affected himself.

He was doubly delighted when, murmuring in his ear words that he had only heard on the web, the ER doctor described the fondling that she expected from him in return. Thus he came to know parts of the feminine anatomy that hasty youths seldom take the time to explore and to award the attention they deserve. He found the lesson so valuable that he had the hostess repeat it, the better to memorize it, and he was no less delighted the second time round by the marvels he discovered. Nor was the ER doctor.

That night, Ari slept ten hours through. The following nights as well. During the day, he didn't for a moment forget to whom he had given his heart. On the contrary, once the ER doctor had left for work, he installed himself in front of the computer to look for jokes that would make Moli laugh. It's true, he said, that every cloud has a silver lining. If I had stayed on the train, I would never have known that you have to make a woman laugh, or what pleases her most in bed, and I would perhaps have lost Moli once I'd found her.

The ER doctor sheltered and entertained Ari until his ankle was no longer swollen and he could again walk without crutches, as happy with the care he'd offered her as he was for hers. Only one concern obsessed our onetime prince-in-waiting: that his hostess might want to hold him back and that he would be leaving her burdened with the responsibility for a broken heart.

He needn't have worried. On the fourteenth night, the ER doctor informed him that she had reserved him a seat on the bus leaving the next morning for the capital. She had also purchased a gift for her brother the deputy.

"You will give it to him in person," she said. "He will not receive it otherwise, busy as he is. You will tell him that you are my patient, and nothing else. He's as prejudiced as my neighbours, and the capital has done nothing to appease his bigotry. Nor his pretensions. On the contrary, they have worsened since he became an important player in national politics, and he behaves as if Providence had elected him as the conscience of the nation. Whatever he says, don't contradict him. If you want him to call the director of the Conservatory, you must applaud his sermons and his fantasies. If he's a sycophant when he wants to get his way, and knows how sycophancy can intoxicate you when you take it straight, he has remained as vulnerable as a child to flattery."

12

ARI ARRIVED AT THE CAPITAL, head full of jokes to make his loved one laugh, along with some subtle sensual manoeuvres to give her pleasure. With the help of his map, he found the Conservatory and made the rounds of the hotels and rooming houses that the groaner on the train had singled out. Moli was living at none of them. But he was again breathing the same air as she was, and that was enough to revive his hope and joy. He rented a room, and the next day, he went early to the office of the ER doctor's brother.

The deputy was a few years older than his sister, and had the bland face of an uncle rather than the tense and austere appearance of the bigot the ER doctor had described to him. He thanked Ari for having delivered his sister's present, then he asked what his intentions were concerning the lady he was seeking.

"To make her my wife and the mother of my children, Mister Deputy, sir," Ari replied, thinking it would be to his advantage under the circumstances to show him due respect.

"I'm happy to hear that," the deputy said. "Nowadays young men think only of their own pleasure, and have no regard for the virtue of women and the future of the family. I will make it my duty to discover the whereabouts of your fiancée. If she wants to be an actress, she must be as sturdily built as you."

"She is a bouquet of graces and virtues, Mister Deputy. One cannot set eyes on her without being overcome."

"Make many children, my boy. Our country needs them. All the more so now that this foreign brood that has installed itself in our land are reproducing like cockroaches."

Ari wanted to tell him that human history was only a succession of migrations, but the ER doctor had warned him not to contradict her brother. Measuring his words and the tone of his voice, he replied:

"Yes, Mister Deputy."

"Tell me about yourself. Do you want to be an actor as well? Is that why your parents aren't helping you to find your fiancée?"

Ari told him what his mother had done, as he had related it to the groaner on the train, to the hermit, and to the ER doctor, expecting the deputy to show him as much understanding as they did. Imagine his astonishment when the latter said to him:

"I thought there was something odd about your story. I asked my sister how it was that he didn't know where to find his fiancée or that his father was not helping him to locate her? If the barley king had called, the prime minister himself would have contacted the director of the Conservatory to get her location. My sister just answered that she didn't know why your father had not done so; she lied to me. That doesn't surprise me, given the kind of life she leads."

"Your sister did not lie to you, Mister Deputy, I'm the one who did not tell her the whole truth," Ari said, himself lying, so as to defend the ER doctor. "But I have so much respect for you that I could never hide anything from you. You are not only the star of your party, but my idol as well. To tell you the whole truth, I wanted to study history. Your actions and your words, however, have persuaded me that I must rather turn toward the future, and I have decided to embark upon political science."

Flattered, the deputy excused himself for having been carried away.

"I was troubled by your story," he said. "How can a child inflict such pain on the one who had given him life? I wondered. Has he lost the fear of God? Does he not know, lover of history that he is, that after having conquered the world to distance himself from his mother, because she demanded too high a price for having carried him in her breast, Alexander the Great died of remorse at the age of 33? Because you cannot escape the one who has given you life, my boy. Wherever we go, as far as our legs may carry us, we all live with our mother, always. In our heads."

Ari knew that Alexander the Great had not been overcome by remorse. Some historians even thought that his own mother had had him poisoned. But again, he did not dare contradict the deputy who, in full flight, said:

"I'm glad that the director of the Conservatory did not know the whereabouts of your friend. I would never have forgiven myself if I had found her for you and added to your mother's pain by condemning her prince to a premature death. And all that for an actress. Ask any man who has had the misfortune to fall in love with one of these professional temptresses, my boy. Their charms are like their performances, promising paradise and raising the curtain on hell. Only a mother's love is constant in what it promises. And its flame is enormous, eternal. Be thankful for it rather than distancing yourself from it. Your mother wanted to save you from what is irreparable. Because she knew that these ignoble temptresses have only one role in mind, that which the Evil One accords them in those shameful masquerades that sap morality and contribute to humanity's decline. And should it happen that one of them sometimes accepts the roles of spouse and mother, she will abandon them as soon as the Evil One promises her another, more flamboyant. I say this for your own good, young man. You are the descendant of an illustrious line. Do it honour, resist mirages, defend the ideals of our glorious race."

Disturbed by the turn his meeting with the deputy had taken, this time Ari could not contain himself.

"You are not thinking of my well-being," he said. "You fear my mother. You know her reputation and you're afraid she will put your eyes out if you help me."

The deputy summoned his bodyguard before Ari could end his rebuke. And when the bodyguard appeared, his boss ordered him to throw the little brat out.

13

A RI WAS IN SUCH A STATE that he wanted to howl out his rage right there on the sidewalk. Instead, he took shelter in a phone booth, and called his grandmother.

"What did you expect after your stupid outburst?" she said when he'd done with venting his frustration. "The ER doctor had warned you: don't contradict him."

"I couldn't just ignore such hypocrisy, granny."

"And what did you gain? Did you tell him where you were staying?"

"Didn't get the chance."

"So much the better. To gain favour with your mother, he would have called to give her the name of the hotel. So how are you going to find Moli now?"

"I met someone in the train who might help me."

The groaner's store was right nearby. But Ari had a good idea of what he would want in exchange. As he still had enough money to last five days, he decided to hang out in front of the Conservatory. Sooner or later, Moli would come to register.

The Conservatory was situated at the end of a vast square, facing the monument to the Unknown Soldier, surrounded by a fountain, where, it was said, on moonless nights, you could see the shades leaning in to drink. During the day the place was teeming with tourists and shoppers, and handsome Ari found himself being stared at from the moment he arrived. As usual, he thought that he was being mistaken for someone else, that something was hanging from his nose, or that he'd forgotten to zip up his fly. Then men accosted him, murmuring indecent propositions, and he changed his location three times, without ever taking his eyes off the Conservatory entrance.

That is how he spent his day, hidden in one corner or the other, observing the young people who went in and out of the Conservatory, not even daring to slake his thirst at the fountain of returning ghosts, so that he wouldn't have to abandon his post to pee.

Then, in the middle of the afternoon, two policemen approached him. For a good ten years, anyone who had something to get off his chest did so by slathering the walls with his anger. And when the capital's walls were all covered with graffiti, those with a grudge took it out on the buildings and official monuments, with explosives. And so the policemen began by searching Ari. Finding nothing suspicious on him, they asked him why he was loitering there. He replied that he was waiting his turn to sign up at the Conservatory, which was not hard to believe, with his drop-dead looks. But when the policemen continued to observe him from afar, he had no choice but to enter the building.

In the foyer, there were photos of former students, whose names were more or less covered over with the dust of oblivion, and he had to pretend to be interested in them until closing time without anyone asking him what he wanted. When he finally emerged, he went to eat and drink, then returned to the hotel, reread the note that Moli had left for him, and went to sleep, lulled by nostalgia.

The next morning, he left the hotel without his jacket. He bought himself a cap to hide his hair and his eyes, picked up a pile of circulars in a store, and posted himself in front of the Conservatory to distribute them to passersby, proud of having found such an ingenious way to deceive the policemen.

14

ON THE MORNING of the last day for registering, Ari was getting ready to leave for the Conservatory, when someone knocked on the door of his room. Who could it be, if not Moli? She had learned that he'd arrived in the capital, and called all the hotels to find him. And so, his heart pounding, he opened the door. And saw his mother, the barley queen.

"What a pretty love nest," she said as she entered, her limp hair, her pale lips, her black dress and her flat shoes making her look slight and fragile. "Do you eat at a soup kitchen? I'm being spoiled as well. Providence has blessed me with a son who feeds me well with bitterness and worry."

She choked back a sob.

"How can you screw her while your parents are shedding tears of blood?" she said. *"You will honour your father and your mother.* Has she so muddled your brain that you've forgotten that whoever transgresses this commandment will find nothing along his path but pitfalls placed there by the Eternal One? That a mother, however demanding and possessive she may be, is sacred, and that he who wounds her will be condemned to bear within him a heart forever shattered? I too was rebellious at your age. That's nature's way. Without the restiveness of each new generation, we would still be living in caves. That is why western civilization, which boasts the greatest number of malcontents, is the most advanced. But there are limits, lines you cannot cross without attracting heaven's wrath. Since your departure, your father has been in mourning, convinced that he will never see you again. He doesn't eat, he neglects his affairs and his dress, he shuts himself in your room as if you were dead and buried there, and he comes out each time older than when he went in. When I look at him, a father with such a big and sick heart, I sometimes regret having brought you into the world. Ah, why do you force me to say such things, my angel?" Then, between sobs: "Stop me. I don't know any more what I'm saying."

Even though he held her responsible, Ari couldn't see his mother so distraught without being touched. He held her in his arms and promised to speak to his father.

"I am so comforted to hear you say that," she said. "He's a weak and sensitive man, who needs constant reassurance, coaxing. Like your brother. Fortunately, you take after me. Ah, if you knew how I've missed you. The joy I feel when I see you. My prince. My light. My life."

Eager to leave for the Conservatory, Ari didn't protest when she said they were made from the same cloth. Instead he took up the phone to call his father. But his mother stopped him. To come back to himself, she said, his father needed to see him, to touch him.

"I will not return to the kingdom," Ari replied.

"You must, my love. And not just for your father. You must also free your conscience, talk with him, man to man, to receive his blessing."

"Very well, I will go to see him next week."

"And if his heart gives out in the meantime? How could you live, knowing that you were the cause of his death? What will you say to defend yourself when you find yourself standing before the court of a heavenly judge? I beg you, I can no longer bear the sound of his lamentations. Do you want me to get down on my knees?"

"Stop, mother. Get up, please."

"Then tell me that you'll come back with me. I will ask you for nothing more, may God be my witness. When you will have spoken to your father and been given his blessing, I will agree to whatever decision you want to impose on me. If not," she added, wooing him and threatening him in the same breath, "I will be pitiless. Your whore and you will have me as a demon on your backs, for the rest of your lives."

Her grudges were deep-rooted and she was merciless with anyone who blocked her way. Ari knew it. But rather than intimidating him, he mother's threats sharpened his resentment of her, and he said:

"My father would not be in this state if you had not driven away Moli."

"I was working in your best interest."

"I loved her."

"She was only leading you on."

"Why can you not accept any feeling that doesn't accord with your own ambitions and prejudices?"

"I know women, and I know what they're capable of."

"Of course, you know everything. The others are only morons and have to defer to your judgments and your desires. Well, you won't choose my destiny as well. I've come to the capital to find the girl I love. And who loves me. Because, believe it or not, you're not the only woman who has a heart. And if you had one, instead of making me feel guilty about my father, you would have brought him with you. We would have explained ourselves, here and now. Why did he not come with you, if he wanted so much to see me, to touch me? Did you veto that, too? I'd love to ask him that. And to make him understand, once and for all, that I may be an idiot, but I'm also an adult. And as an adult, I have the right to find my own way. And you should respect my decision."

"Adult?" his mother cried out, not caring whether she was being heard all over the hotel. "I still feel the blows you dealt me in my womb, the soreness at the tips of my breasts when you sucked on them, the sleepless nights I spent at your bedside when, at the age of two, you caught meningitis. You're asking me to forget all that, and for a whore? You could be fifty years old, have fifty wives and fifty children, and I would feel it still. I am a mother! You hear me? A mother! The void you left here, in the middle of my body, only the sight of your face and the sound of your voice could fill it. You will never be able to hide from that. Get this into your head. There are debts that not even an entire life can ever pay off. And the life I gave you is the first and the biggest of all."

Drained, she again dissolved in tears, and only stopped crying when her son promised to go and get her later at her hotel, and to return with her to the barley kingdom, for a day or two.

15

♦

WHEN ARI ARRIVED at the Conservatory, rather than lurking in a corner he presented himself at the reception desk, where he learned that Moli had arrived to register early in the morning, and that the auditions would take place in one month. Though he appealed to them to give him her address, they refused to do so and he left, cursing his mother, who had arrived at his room that morning when he would have finally been able to find his beloved.

What to do now? Ask the groaner to help him? And if he insisted that he move in with him and sleep in the same bed? He suddenly remembered his mother's promise. Once you've talked to your father and received his blessing, she had said, I will respect any decision you want to impose on me. It was simple, he would return to the kingdom for two days and, as the deputy had said, after a phone call from the barley king, the prime minister himself would call the Conservatory to get him Moli's address.

And so he went to the luxury hotel where his mother was staying. But she wasn't in her suite. Ari had told her that he'd join her at the end of the day, believing that he would have to monitor the comings and goings at the Conservatory until registrations were complete. Fortunately, the hotel receptionist was more helpful than the one at the theatre school. When Ari told him that he was the son of the barley queen, the man informed him that Madame was dining in the ground floor restaurant, and accompanied him to the entrance.

Ari went no further.

The barley queen was indeed dining there, with two waiters stationed nearby, ready to jump at the slightest signal. But the barley queen was not dining alone. She was dining with the beer king, and was not in the least sad or tearful. On the contrary, she was wearing her hair in a crown and her most beautiful jewels, her lips were as scarlet as her décolleté dress, and she was laughing merrily at what her companion was telling her.

He had to walk for a long time in order to bring under control the anger inspired by the sight of his mother dining and laughing with the man she wanted to be her prince's father-in-law. And he thought he'd made her change her mind. His granny was right – he might as well try to redraw her palm lines.

What made things even worse was that he could not go back to his hotel and deal with his resentment in his room. His mother would be coming to find him there. Nor could he change his hotel. He would have to again write his name in the register, and stubborn as she was, his mother would once more ferret him out. Where was he going to sleep for a whole month, attend to his needs, perform his ablutions? Worse still. Beautiful as she was, many men must be circling around Moli. Believing that her prince was lost forever, the longer it took for him to find her, the more he risked finding her in the consoling arms of another.

Haunted by this new anxiety, he wandered the streets, stopping only to call his father and inform him of his mother's duplicity, then at the end of the day walking into the store managed by the groaner.

He walked in and out three times. Immediately attracting all eyes, some salesgirls, seduced at first by his beauty, ended up finding his behaviour suspicious, and called the security guard. Who in turn called the police. The same ones who had asked Ari why he was surveying the entrance to the Conservatory. They had not forgotten his drop-dead looks. As they themselves were ugly, and because of their ugliness could not accept that someone could be so beautiful, they wanted to take him to the police station and to mess up his face.

"I'm a friend of the manager," he said.

Aware of the manager's inclinations, the guard called his boss. Who arrived, saying:

"The barley prince! Thank heavens, he's alive!"

He led Ari to his office, and when Ari finished recounting all his misadventures since they had parted company on the train, the man said:

"You'll sleep in my house, big boy. If you're nice, I'll call the director of the Conservatory tomorrow morning."

Then he moved quickly to finish up his work, whistling happily.

To hide his discomfort, Ari had turned his back, and was facing a window. There he saw on the sidewalk facing him two girls walking arm in arm, with small lanterns hanging at their necks.

"I'll be right back," he told the groaner, and rushed out of the office.

16

Neither of the two girls looked anything like Moli. He just wanted to catch up with them in order to ask who'd given them the idea for the lanterns, and if it was Moli, where they had encountered her. But by the time he had exited the store and crossed the street, they had disappeared. Ari went into a shop here, explored an alleyway there. But in vain.

He did not lose hope. Moli must be preparing for her audition at the capital's cemetery, he thought to himself. That's where the two girls saw her with her lantern.

He consulted the city map.

There were three cemeteries in the capital.

The nearest was the most ancient and the smallest. You could see all the graves from the street, and Ari concluded that Moli would not be preparing her test there, in full view of passersby and nearby buildings.

The second cemetery was farther off, three times bigger, and the streets surrounding it were deserted. Except for one old tramp who was heading that way as well, breaking the silence with the cart that he was laboriously dragging behind him. He asked Ari to help him, and it was only when he took hold of one of the two shafts that he saw that the cart contained the body of another tramp.

"I can't leave him in the street, at the mercy of the dogs," the man said.

Still, he had to leave the corpse at the entrance: the cemetery was surrounded by high walls, and its tall iron gate was locked up for the night.

All that way for nothing, Ari thought. Then he ran to find a taxi.

The third cemetery was on the western edge of the city. It was more isolated than the first, ten times larger than the second, and had neither a wall nor a gate. It was however, so remote it was impossible that Moli would come there every night to rehearse her text. Ari only realized this when he got out of the taxi. He decided to take a look anyway, just to be on the safe side.

The terrain was flat, the night dark, and he would have seen a lantern glow at the other end of the cemetery. There was nothing.

He was about to turn around when three men passed by in silence a few steps away. Curious, Ari hid himself to see what they were up to, but a gunshot burst out and the men scattered like rats.

Crouched behind a mausoleum, Ari didn't move, while steps approached, gravel crunching on the path.

"I see you, the fourth one, behind that tomb!" a man cried, who it would appear saw better in the darkness than Ari. "Come out of there, you dirty zealot, or I'll shoot!"

Ari came out of his hiding place, saying:

"I'm not with them, sir. I don't even know why you called them zealots."

"So what are you doing here at this hour?"

The man was the cemetery watchman, and when Ari told him about Moli, his mother's visit, and the two girls wearing lanterns around their necks, his story inspired such pity in the listener that he invited him to spend the night in his cabin, as there were no more taxis or buses at that hour and the cemetery was too far from the centre of town for him to return on foot. He even offered Ari something to eat, explaining that he called zealots the members of the radical fringe of the conservative party. Under cover of night, they came with hammers to demolish the statues decorating the tombs, especially those with breasts. And those acts of vandalism and profanation had become more frequent since the right had come to power.

"The only nudity they tolerate is that of skeletons," the watchman said. "Probably because they don't display any breasts or sexual organs. Eat, my boy, eat."

Ari would have liked to eat, but a few inches from his plate, on a square of blue velvet, sat a skull with only six teeth remaining, one of them gold.

"That's my wife's skull," the watchman said. "I set it on the table at supper time and tell her about my day."

Then, stroking the skull:

"Can you do something, little dear, to help this nice boy find his sweetheart before she's stolen away?"

Ari went back to the square on the first bus the next morning, and searched all day, in vain, for the two girls with the lanterns. To rest, he leaned against a wall. When the policemen got near, he flung himself into a store. And once the stores were closed and the square emptied of people, but not of policemen, he took shelter under a bridge.

When he wakened, he went into a fast-food restaurant to urinate and get washed. But when it came time to order breakfast, he found that his pockets were empty. He had been robbed of everything while he slept, even Moli's letter, and exhausted as he was, he'd been aware of nothing.

He was so hungry that he didn't scan the crowd that morning. Like the beggars who, humble as pigeons, scanned the ground for something to eat or smoke, he spent his time looking for a coin with which he might phone his grandmother and ask her to telegraph a bit of money. There was, of course, the soup kitchen, but the barley queen might pass by while he was standing in line. He would rather sleep with the groaner than see his mother laugh at his wretched state, brought about by his "whore."

And so he went back to the department store, waited for the elevator to go up to the manager's office, and when the door opened on the elevator's occupants, he suddenly saw a ray of light in the darkness that had engulfed him.

"My love!" cried the ray of light. "I've just bought my first pair of sheets, and I was imagining that I was trying them out with you!"

They threw themselves into each other's arms and remained for a long moment in an embrace so touching that the other women merging from the elevator's cabin had their eyes brimming with water.

17

MOLI HAD ALSO BOUGHT three cushions, some perfumed candles, and a reproduction of Matisse's *Red Fish*. But when she went back to her small furnished room, before putting things away she gave Ari, who was famished, something to eat. And while he feasted, she told him about her troubles since coming to the capital.

She had very little money, no particular skills, and the jobs she'd been offered barely covered her food and rent. She also had to clothe herself and soon pay her school fees. However, she had studied dance, and a Conservatory student she'd met in a café brought her to Harem, a cabaret offering striptease shows where she could earn in one week what young people working in fast-food restaurants were paid in a month.

No sooner had he shaken her hand than the owner of Harem asked her to take off her clothes, examined her from head to toe, then, without the least hint of lechery in his voice, said: "We'll have to find you a name as seductive as your ass. Your friend had a treble clef tattooed around her navel. As soon as I saw it, I told her: 'Your name will be Melody, and the theme of your performance will be Melody fiddling with her flute.'"

He thought for a moment. "I love this part of my job – finding the concept. Very important, the concept."

He thought a little more. "It'll come. These are the mysteries of creation. You're having a crap, and wham – a flash! Put your bra and underpants back on, and let's see what we can do. Maybe it will come while I watch you dancing."

Moli put back on her bra and underpants.

"I introduce you," the man said. "*And now, the last and the freshest flower in your harem – Moli!* Or the name I'll have found. The song begins, you come on stage …"

Moli was proud of her body, and, as we've said, not at all timid. But the idea of dancing at ten o'clock in the morning, in underpants and on an empty stomach, in front of a stranger, made her so nervous that she could hardly move.

"Who taught you to dance, a bear trainer?" the Harem's owner said with a snigger.

He climbed onstage. "Look closely. I won't do it twice."

He applied himself to demonstrating the secrets of erotic dancing with such clumsiness that once Moli got over her embarrassment, the hardest thing was to suppress her laughter.

"Imagine the scene," she told Ari. "A fat, pot-bellied fifty-year-old, as well versed in choreography as a butcher is in heart surgery, mimicking the contortions of a stripper, at times bending back around the metal pole and juddering his breasts, at times leaning forwards and wriggling his ass. 'That's seduction,' he said, then he asked me to imitate his movements."

"That's better," he said, "but you have to let yourself go more. Imagine you're in your bedroom, dancing for your boyfriend. You must have one."

Moli talked about Ari, their nights at the cemetery, and the shrew who'd put an end to all that.

Rather than being moved, the man scolded her for not having told him about it earlier. "It will be a fabulous number. The lanterns. The cemetery … Tristana! That's your stage name. Tristana the sobbing widow. Every number is made up of three dances. In the first, you're in your room, alone with your memories. In the second, you're visiting your boyfriend's grave and you give him a farewell dance, because you just can't live without his cock."

This time Moli refused to obey. Her Ari was very much alive, and such a number might bring bad luck. But the Harem's owner considered his concept brilliant and refused to find another. "Men," he said, "love imagining a fuck with ladies desperate for cock, like widows and divorcees. We could do a number so exciting that all the clients will want to invite you to their tables to console you. You could pay off your first year at the Conservatory in two months. Besides, your mourning will camouflage your stiffness and your blunders, and there'll be lots of them at first. So make up your mind. I have other things to do. You're Tristana the widow, or you're out the door."

That was how he succeeded in imposing his concept on Moli. Then he threw a tantrum when she didn't execute a move the way he wanted. "Start again," he said, more and more short of breath, his body exuding bursts of sour sweat. Until he stretched out on the floor to show her how, in the third act, wearing no more than her longing for a cock, she had to end her number.

"Lying on your back, your slit so close to their faces that they could lick it, you caress yourself as if you were caressing your dream of becoming a star," he said, his legs pumping the air and his head shifting from side to side, in a simulation of female masturbation so grotesque that this time, Moli couldn't hold back her laughter.

The man shot her the darkest of grimaces. Like all those who adore laughing at others, he couldn't tolerate that someone might amuse herself at his expense. He even refused the hand she held out to help him to get up. And when he was finally on his feet, he told her to go and shave her pubis. He had to think about the costume and the music. Afterward, he would show her how to dance on tables.

"I shaved my pubis," Moli said. "My nudity has become a disguise, and five nights a week I play the widow, shedding real tears onto the grave of a dream I thought had vanished forever."

71

18

MOLI'S TEARS HAD ALSO LURED women to Harem, and some of those who were mourning a loved one went out in public with a lantern around their necks. But Ari could not rejoice at the success of his beloved. He had never seen her naked, and his heart twinged at the idea that others were ogling her most intimate parts and maybe even groping them. He promised himself to find work as soon as possible, so Moli wouldn't have to practise this profession. Then he called his grandmother to tell her that his stint of misery had come to an end.

Moli had the day off, and they spent the evening together, planning for the future and remembering with tenderness their first meeting and the nocturnal rehearsals that followed, each one enlivening their memories with some amusing detail missing from the other's account. Melody, the flute dancer, who was in her second year at the Conservatory, was now helping Moli to prepare for her audition. She had also introduced her to other students and a few professors as well, most of them actors whose very names fed one's dreams.

"It's a ruthless world, the competition is fierce, and your contacts are extremely important, you need them if you want to succeed," Moli explained, with perfect frankness.

Unlike Ari, she was no more surprised at the impact her beauty had on people than she doubted her own talent, convinced that sooner or later it would lead her out of anonymity and make her a star.

"I grew up poor," she said. "I had nothing but my dreams. And dreams are strong in people who have nothing."

If there remained in Ari's mind the slightest temptation to go back and see the groaner, her words did away with it for good. He just had to find work to save Moli from undressing every night before a bunch of voyeurs, and himself from taking the money that she needed to fulfil her dream.

"Melody has access to the fashion world," she told him. "She and I could be models if we were five centimetres taller and five kilos lighter. You, on the other hand, are exactly the kind of dark and handsome type they want. You'll earn ten times more than a store clerk, and you'll have plenty of time to further your studies."

Ari replied that he hated being photographed. And he was afraid his mother would see his picture in a magazine and be able to find him.

The evening was well advanced by the time they lay down on Moli's new sheets for the first time. And while the distant stars smiled down through the window at their happiness, Ari served up to his beloved some of the caresses he had picked up from the ER doctor. Moli was delighted, but once again she pushed him away when he wanted to enter her. Ari then tried to make her laugh – when a woman laughs, the hermit had said, you can do what you want with her – but it was a lost cause. Moli didn't want to get pregnant. She had before her four years at the Conservatory. How could she get through them if, in addition to her studies, there was work and a child?

"I'll work," Ari said. "You'll just have to study and breast feed the baby."

Moli burst out laughing.

"Usually, it's the girl who wants the child and the guy who takes off."

"I was thinking that if you were carrying mine, my mother would have no choice but to bless our union."

Moli stopped laughing.

"I think we're going to have our first argument."

"Why do you say that?"

"You don't want to be a model for fear that your mother will see your picture in a magazine. You want to make me pregnant just to win her over. You're still under her thumb, Ari, she's controlling you. Think about it."

He wanted to reconcile his mother in order to fully live his love. Because knowing that his father was suffering because of their estrangement cast a shadow even over this day of reunion and happiness. But he promised to clear his mind of the barley queen and to speak no more of children. Then, unable to separate himself from Moli in his sleep, he watched her sleeping and ran to fix breakfast as soon as she opened her eyes.

"You can't look for work in the clothes you've been wearing for a month," she said when they'd finished eating.

She led him to a store, where she picked out some pants, a jacket, a dress shirt, and a pair of shoes, asking him to try on each item, so she could judge the effect. She added socks and underwear, then stopped at the pharmacy to buy a box of condoms. As for Ari, he noted on a piece of paper the price of each article, so he could reimburse her once he found a job.

19

WHEN HE ARRIVED at the department store, he was sporting his most luminous smile. Not the groaner.

"Since we met on the train," he said, "I've been dreaming of seeing you naked in my bed, of peeling an orange and feeding it to you, section by section. But as soon as you appear, pouf! you vanish. Enough. You've left me in the lurch three times. Either you strip down here and now, or you get out of my sight forever."

"I can do neither one nor the other," Ari replied. "On the one hand because I only love Moli, who I've finally found. On the other hand, because I need to earn my living, and you promised me a job."

"Why are you doing this to me?" the groaner moaned. "We were going to look for your friend together. Not only did you not keep your word, you want to force your pretty face on me all day long without my being able to touch it? No. I don't want to spend all day groaning."

"That's too bad," Ari said. "I was intending to ask you to be the godfather of our first child."

"Is that true?" the groaner asked, moved.

"You're the only friend I have in the capital. And it's very much thanks to you that I found Moli."

"You must absolutely find a job. A child costs a lot of money. Unfortunately, I can only hire you for the moment as a shelf filler."

"What's a shelf filler?"

"You transport boxes from the warehouse to the shelves. With a trolley, of course, so as not to hurt your back, and with gloves to protect your pretty hands. You then open the boxes with a little box cutter, you take out the articles, and you place them carefully on the shelves. It's not very rewarding, the salary is modest, but you'll wear some very manly coveralls, and a matching helmet to protect your lovely head. In addition to which, from the first day, you'll have the right to a twenty percent reduction on anything you buy at the store. That will be especially advantageous for a new household, there are a thousand things to buy, and Moli, like any woman, must hate empty rooms. As for the nursery, I'll take care of that myself when the time comes."

Ari began to work the next day, charming all his coworkers with his good looks and his friendly manner. Still, Moli did not leave Harem. She wanted first to put aside enough money to pay for her education. And so she continued to dance and to shed tears over the grave of her man, knowing now that he was waiting for her at the exit so she wouldn't have to return home alone at night, that he would serve her a supper he'd cooked, that once her stomach was full, he would cater to the other parts of her body, and she would go to sleep, entirely refreshed. In short, she passed her audition, and when she learned she was accepted, Ari, who had received his first paycheque, organized a celebration, to which he invited the groaner and some of Moli's friends. They all bandied about the gossip actors love, then talked of the zealots who, after having won the cancellation of a serial featuring a character who was gay, were now insisting that the National Theatre withdraw productions of Aristophanes' *Lysistrata* and Molière's *Tartuffe*. "If they keep that up," they said, "there won't be a single theatre open by the time we've finished our studies, and nothing left on television but sermons."

"Stop your worrying," the groaner said. "They only represent ten percent of the population."

"But that ten percent is clinging to beliefs no one can budge," Ari remarked. "And people with no doubts are the most dangerous," he added, basing himself on his historical knowledge and his personal experience, thinking in particular of his mother.

"How can you worship a divinity you've never seen, and despise your own body and its desires?" Moli asked.

"These are tortured souls who can't bear the idea of being an ephemeral bundle of flesh," claimed some.

"They're not tortured, they're vain," argued others. "Vain beings who're more interested in their immortality than in the truth."

Enlivened by the wine, they imagined a show that would denounce the zealots, they chanted revolutionary songs, they kept the party going until late in the night.

"I've never been so happy," Moli said, after the guests had left. "I'm going to study at the Conservatory and I have a man that all the women envy me. You must have seen how they were all eating you up with their eyes."

Ari, who was clearing the table, blushed like a child, and Moli was overcome with tenderness.

"Leave the dishes, we'll deal with them tomorrow," she said, dimming the light. "I want to play the rich old actress with her gigolo."

And thus they spent their first month, Ari living only for the moment when he would once again see his Moli, and she delighting him with her skill in transforming the simplest acts into small celebrations, whether it be in lovemaking, or a visit to a thrift store, or a café meal with their friends, friends more and more fearful of the zealots who were now demanding that the government declare sperms to be autonomous individuals and that it ban all forms of contraception.

When he received his second paycheque, Ari called his grandmother to tell her that he could now repay the money that she'd given him. She replied that he should use it to sign up, as well, for an academic course. Surely he hadn't renounced his inheritance just to line up trinkets on shelves.

The next day, Ari picked up history programs from two universities in the capital, studied them all evening, and when Moli came home from work, rather than making love to her, he talked about historiographic problems, analyses, and the synthesis of spatio-temporal contexts, just as a child would rattle on about rides at an amusement park that he was going to visit.

But as everyone knows, desires do not alone shape our futures, and a banal incident would soon come along to sabotage their plans.

20

WITH HIS CUTTER, he was opening a box in the kitchenware section of the department store, when a zealot and his wife approached to check out the trays lined up on a shelf. Round, oval, and rectangular trays, with or without handles, in melamine or plastic of every colour, wood and stainless steel as well, and even synthetic leather.

The box that Ari had just opened contained teak trays with folding legs. He had already set one aside for his sweetheart's breakfasts in bed, and lifting out another, he said to the zealot:

"Take this one, sir. It's very practical for serving Madame her breakfast in bed."

The zealot shot him a furious look and then stalked off with his wife, saying:

"He laughs best who laughs last!"

Five minutes later he came back with the manager, who asked Ari to apologize to the gentleman.

"Apologize for what?"

"For what you said."

"I was only suggesting ..."

"It's for the salespeople to serve the clients," the groaner said, interrupting and raising his voice, to the delight of the zealot. "Your job is to fill the shelves, and nothing more. So apologize for your offence."

"But I committed no offence."

"My wife was a witness," the zealot shouted, as a crowd gathered. "Because she was not dressed like a harlot, he spoke of her with a sneer on his face."

"That's not true," Ari protested.

"And to add insult to injury," the zealot said, "he threatened me with a box cutter when I got angry."

"Not true!" poor Ari repeated. "I was holding the cutter because I was opening boxes, but I never threatened him with it. Say something, Madame. Did I threaten your husband? Was I laughing at you?"

"Leave her alone!" the zealot cried. "You're dealing with me! Or are you afraid to have it out with a real man!"

Now it was the groaner's turn to lose his cool.

"What are you insinuating, sir?"

"You'll soon find out," the zealot replied, turning his back.

The groaner caught up with him, begged him to be patient for a moment, came back to Ari, and lowering his voice, said:

"I know you're not a cutter-wielding madman. But you still suggested that he serve his wife breakfast in bed."

"So?"

"Don't make a mistake that will haunt you all your life. Please apologize."

"For suggesting that he serve his wife breakfast in bed?"

"Yes."

"That's ridiculous."

"I know, my boy. But these jerks do not think like you and me."

"Maybe it's time they changed their attitude."

"Not so loud, idiot!"

Too late, everyone had heard Ari. And while some applauded him, the zealot strode away, ignoring the groaner's pleas to let him have a few more words with his employee.

An hour later, about fifty zealots were demonstrating in front of the store, chanting slogans and urging people to take their business elsewhere.

The groaner said to Ari:

"I'm going to have to suspend you, without pay, until the storm has blown over, otherwise they'll wreck my store."

Ari left by the service door while the groaner informed the demonstrators that he had fired the culprit. But they refused to leave.

"He insulted our brother," they said. "He humiliated him in front of his wife and a crowd of people. He even attacked him with a knife. We won't leave until your employee publicly apologizes for his offence."

21

WHEN MOLI LEARNED that her beloved had been fired, and why, she called her friends, they contacted their own friends, and with the help of the telephone and social media they organized a counter demonstration for the next day in front of the groaner's store.

"Why make the situation worse?" Ari said. "I'll be rehired once the zealots leave."

"It's not just your job," Moli replied. "The zealot's response to your suggestion for a platter with folding legs is symptomatic of a much more widespread evil. Those fanatics keep repeating that God is love, but they see other people through the prism of hate. A hatred of everything that is different and liable to cast doubt on their faith. The proof: Your zealot, because he believes women were created to serve men, immediately interpreted your suggestion as an attack on his values and beliefs."

"Do you think that in taunting him, you're going to make him change his mind?"

"I don't want to change anyone. They're the ones who want us to conform to their ideology. And if we do nothing – history can bear witness to this – they will continue to light fires until we give in. You said it yourself, at my party. They could even ban every kind of performance, as the Christians did for a thousand years, after Alexandria's fall. Yes or no?"

"Yes."

"So why don't you want to demonstrate with us? What are you really afraid of? That there will be cameras and your mother will see you on the news? I thought that you'd put her out of your mind."

Ari went with Moli to the counter-demonstration. As much so as not to lose her respect as to show his mother that he was completely free of her. And there were plenty of cameras on the square to transmit the message. Not only those of the television networks that the organizers of the counter-demonstration had alerted. Everyone, or almost , had a cell phone, all the phones were now equipped with a camera, and their owners, as soon as they got home, for the most part rushed to their computers, to post on the Internet the images they had captured.

Here are a few examples.

Their banners waving in the air, calling for justice, repentance, and respect, fifty or so zealots are congregated in front of the groaner's department store. The groaner is nowhere in sight.

A procession of more than two hundred people, led by Moli, Ari, and a few show business celebrities, march through the square, brandishing banners that say: *Down with the cult of sin and prohibitions! Lovers of breakfast in bed, unite!* – and other similar slogans.

The parade comes to a halt.

The zealots close ranks.

Moli puts a megaphone to her mouth and says:

"The boy I love and with whom I want to make my life worked in this store. His salary, while modest, allowed us to eat and to furnish our little nest. But yesterday he was fired. He didn't steal, he wasn't lazy, and all his fellow workers loved him. Why was he fired? He had suggested to a zealot looking for a tray that he buy one with feet to serve his wife breakfast in bed … Who would he have offended with this suggestion to have his livelihood taken away and be asked to repent? Certainly not the wife. I myself am delighted when my man serves me breakfast in bed. And all the women I've talked to have replied that they would be as well. Did he offend God? Is it written somewhere that a man must not serve his wife breakfast in bed? On the contrary, the holy books say that a man must give his wife pleasure. Rather than ask for my man's head, you should congratulate him on following the holy scriptures to the letter. And, like the two of us, give thanks to God every morning for these beautiful instruments of pleasure that he has given us."

With these words, in a sleight of hand long since perfected at Harem, Moli removed her dress to offer herself to all eyes just as God who is love had created her.

"You too, my man, make yourself naked," she said to Ari, as whistles from one side and boos from the other all came together in one chorus. "Shame dwells only in clothing. It is written in the holy books."

"Go on, handsome, shame dwells in clothing!" cried some women to Ari while the zealots promised his bitch and him the fires of Hell."

22

"M-m-mama!" Junior, at the other end of the country, cried.

After Ari's departure, the barley queen, rather than paying more attention to her younger son, berated him, just as she berated her entire entourage, and when she wasn't berating anyone, she gave herself over to lamentation, repeating that no sorrow equalled that of having been betrayed by the flesh of one's flesh. So his mother wouldn't tar him with the same brush, Junior made himself small and consoled himself with the virtual friendships and love relationships of the World Wide Web, praying that the abscess would soon burst. Until the day there appeared on his screen an image of the ungrateful son with his naked strumpet by his side, surrounded by a delirious crowd. *That would burst the boil once and for all*, Junior thought. Seeing these images, the beer king would nevermore want Ari as a son-in-law, and the barley queen would stop talking about uniting the two kingdoms. So:

"M-m-mama!" he cried. "Qu-qu-quick, c-c-ome s-s-see!"

"People like you are a disgrace to humanity!" some bystanders shouted at Moli and her friends, while others fought to get close either to congratulate or to abuse her. Thus the mob was divided into two camps. A clash was inevitable.

It came when a zealot shouted "Burn that bitch," charging Moli and sowing panic. At once, the rioters took advantage of the situation to burst out in a pack onto the square, and in an instant Moli vanished, carried off in the surge. Ari threw himself into the crowd, elbowing and groping his way toward his beloved, to pull her out of the surge, swollen now with the police forces sent to the scene, while grinning idiots here and there mugged for the cameras.

"Did you hear?" the barley queen told her husband. "He serves her breakfast in bed. What the hell does he see in her to reject his own mother and serve this hayseed as if he were her slave? Her face has nothing special except the freshness of youth. Her boobs look as though they've been badly lifted. Her waist – I've had two children – mine is more slender. And she dares to parade in front of the cameras stark naked, with my son in tow, thumbing her nose at me. 'My muff had got the best of your breast! I've won!' Over my dead body, you snake!"

The barley king wanted to reply that this spectacle would never have taken place if she'd let her eldest son get his flings out of his system, but when she was in such a state, his wife was interested in a dialogue that allowed only her to express her opinions. And so he opted for a phone call to his lawyers in the capital, asking them to confirm his son's situation.

No sooner had he hung up than his mother-in-law arrived. She had seen Ari and Moli on television. Also she was well acquainted with her daughter's temperament. As angry and spiteful as mythology's legendary gods, she could, with one phone call – the modern version of their thunder – destroy someone at the other end of the land. And so she rushed to the castle to try and limit the damage.

She began by reminding her daughter of her own youthful escapades. Her daughter replied that her escapades had not prevented her from becoming a queen, and that she became a queen because she had her feet on the ground and didn't fill her head with illusions and fantasies, like her gullible son who swallowed everything that was said to him, even if she had warned him that a woman had more schemes in one pubic hair than did a man in all his muscles. And Junior, who thought that he had burst the cursed abscess, heard his mother conclude:

"But I have not said my last word. I have more tricks and ploys than ten little upstarts. And now that I know where to find her, I'm going to teach her what happens to you when you don't know your place!"

"Daughter," the grandmother said, "there are spells that nothing can ward off. Ari is bewitched by love. And pride as well. You ought to know where such a combination may lead, just look at yourself. If you touch his beloved, blinded by love as he is, you may lose him forever."

"It's all your fault," the barley queen answered. "If you hadn't given him money for the train, he would still be here."

"I don't regret what I did, and I would help him again if he asked. Because he is far from being the gullible boy you imagine. You know it, deep down, you've always known it, and you flattered yourself that he was your mirror image. So think. If he is as stubborn and vindictive as his mother, before you act think twice about what he has done and what he might do if you crush his hopes."

23

ARI EXPECTED HIS MOTHER to be at his door at any moment. Added to this anxiety was a phone call from the groaner informing him that, since the whole city had seen images of Moli in the nude, he couldn't rehire him.

"What a coward!" Moli said. "We should tell the zealots about his homosexuality!"

Ari tried to defend the groaner, but in vain. Moli was convinced that all those insulted by nudity had something to hide, because the body never lies. You can't manipulate and oppress it like you can do to the soul with all its mendacity. And she repeated that a hundred times in the following days, badgered as she was by the media, always on the lookout for a sensational story to capture the imagination of their public, and to keep it asking for more.

"It's written that the Creator drove man and woman out of paradise when they became ashamed of their nudity and wanted to hide it," she said. "It's the zealots who should be ashamed of their acts, not me. My stripping down – I'm repeating this for those who only saw an attack on public decency – my stripping down was neither obscene nor provocative. It was simply an expression of thanks offered to the maker of my body. And so if we have religious freedom, let me acknowledge it in my own way. I allow them to give thanks to their own religion as they please, don't I?"

And so, in this world where the image rules, her public strip-tease made her a celebrity before she had taken a single course at the Conservatory. The left-wing parties were delighted. The owner of Harem as well. The latter because Moli sold out the room every night; the others because they had found their standard bearer. They invited her to all their demonstrations. Moli repeated her spiel, then invited everyone to undress just like her, saying that it was to deride one's body and demonize it that was the real sin.

As for Ari, the more popular Moli became, the more concerned he was. As much for his beloved's security as for the barley queen's reaction. He had not heard from her yet, and he wondered what she was plotting, doubting that she'd decided to throw in the towel and to leave him in peace. On top of this, however much he combed through the classified ads looking for a job, just like the groaner, no one would dare hire him and risk the wrath of the zealots. In fact, a week after Moli's strip-tease on the square, a fire destroyed Harem, but neither the police nor the government dared to accuse anyone, on the pretext that there was no proof and no witnesses.

Moli's rage grew. She had only saved up half of the tuition fees for her first year, and no other club owner wanted to hire her and have his cabaret burn down.

"Because of your stupid job," she told Ari, "I'm not going to be able to pay my fees, and they're going to cancel my registration."

"I didn't want you to demonstrate, and even less that you take off your clothes."

"Because you thought about your mother, and what she would say. Otherwise you'd have stripped down too. After all, you were the victim. I was fighting for you. It's not enough to have convictions, and dreams, you also need the courage to defend them. But you, all you have that's princely is your beauty and grace, and you only strip to make me a child. Even that, you do it to placate your mother. That doesn't make you a man, just a wimp."

That was the only word she had on her lips these days – all men were cowards and wimps, except for those who took off their clothes along with her at the demonstrations – but she had never thrown it in the face of her beloved, or wielded it with such contempt. Rather than reminding her that he had only once talked about impregnating her, and accusing her and her supporters of stripping only to get on TV, because their stripping never achieved anything else, Ari held his peace and waited for Moli to calm down and come to her senses. But his silence and the virtues of patience that he deployed in her presence only exacerbated the girl's rage.

"Why am I still with you?" she said to him one night. "I've had nothing but problems since I met you. Sure, you make me laugh and you're great in bed. But as for the rest, you're as useless as a bell without a clapper. You have nothing to say? Too scared to say what you think, eh?"

"Stop taking everything out on me, my love."

"You can't help me, you bring me bad luck, you shatter my dreams to please your mother, and now you want to shut me up?"

Why was she still talking to him about his mother? He never mentioned her any more, and he had never ever tried to stifle her dreams. On the contrary, with the little money he had, he bought lottery tickets, hoping to win enough to pay for her education. Even when he showed her the darned tickets, Moli only treated him as an enemy.

"I will not sacrifice my dreams and my freedom for anyone," she said. "Even less for a wimp who thinks that lotteries are won by those who need money. Fortunately, I know some men with balls and lots of cash. They're just waiting for a sign from me to support me and to attend to my needs. The barley queen will be delighted to hear that. She's always called me an opportunist and a whore. That's what I am. Run and tell your mommy."

And with these words, she left, slamming the door.

24

HE WAITED FOR MOLI all through the evening and then all night. When there was no sign of her, he called her friends. None of them knew where she was, and all were astonished that she had left him. Except for Melody. In a dry tone of voice, as if she also held him responsible for the loss of her job at Harem, she said:

"Are you stupid or what? She doesn't love you anymore. Cross her out."

Ari hung up, his heart in shreds.

I've done everything I could to spare you this sorrow, but you didn't want to listen, he heard his mother's voice telling him. She wanted to say more, but he chased her away with a groan, then left the apartment to find Moli and reclaim her love. He visited one by one the places she liked to frequent. The thrift stores full of the vintage clothes that Moli loved. The movie theatres where she could see the actresses she dreamed of emulating. The cafés where she liked to observe the customers, in order to build up, she said, a repertoire of characters, something very important for her development as a performer. And for a brief time, the stream of sounds, odours, and images gave him the illusion that nothing had changed, that from one moment to another he would be reunited with his love, that they would have a drink or two, then go home tipsy and throw themselves onto the bed, consumed by desire. And from one place to another, each time he came up empty-handed, he heard his mother's voice berating him for his moments of deception. At first he was able to shoo her away with a groan. But the fewer places there remained for him to search, the more the barley queen's voice imposed itself. *I am your mother*, it said. *Groan all you want, you've left my womb but you will never escape my mind.*

Then, one groan and one café farther on: *Stop your search! You were so love drunk, she thought you'd cater to her every whim with the ease of a deft genie. You couldn't do it, so she's found herself another sucker. Face facts, give up and come back to the castle.*

Another groan and one last café: *Thank god you haven't found her. Not all women are the same breed as your mother. After one or two pregnancies, she'd have looked like a field snubbed by the rain.*

To drown out the barley queen's voice, he bought a bottle of wine and kept on walking, hoping to come upon one of the demonstrations in which Moli participated, because he refused to admit that all was over between him and this girl lodged in every part of his body and his flesh. But if the wine silenced his mother's voice, it did not lessen his suffering, and when, toward midnight, he saw on a deserted square a zealot tearing down a poster featuring a girl in a bathing suit, he threw himself at him, accusing him of having lost him the love of his life, and he would have punched him to death if the other had not managed to escape.

"My poor girl," he said to the poster. "What did he do to you, that idiot?"

Then, trying to patch it up by sticking the pieces back on the wall with his leftover wine:

"He really did a job on you. What's wrong with these people? You don't like to see a girl in a bathing suit? Cross her out. Your man has lost his job? Cross him out. And what about the heart, eh? How do you cross out the heart, the dreams that your beloved has sown in it and sustained? I gave up a kingdom for her. I even learned how to give pleasure to a woman and to make her laugh. Many women flocked around me. But I only wanted to make Moli laugh and give pleasure to her. She was everything to me. Until she became someone else. But I didn't change. I'm as much in love with her as on the first day. My god, it was so good to come back to her every night. To touch and to embrace the one I'd been dreaming of all day long. He was right, the old beekeeper, to retire from the world. My heart too aches at the sight of every loving couple … For certain, I'd know how to find his cabin. It was perched on the highest tree in the forest."

He would have spent the night lamenting his lost love and reconstituting the poster piece by piece, had the zealot not come back, with three accomplices. They rained down blows on him and only stopped when a patrol car passing by made them scurry away.

25

Hᴉs ʙᴇᴀᴛɪɴɢ ᴍᴀᴅᴇ ʜᴇᴀᴅʟɪɴᴇs when the identity of his father became known. The barley king flew to his bedside as soon as he heard the news, and his heart almost failed when he saw how swollen was his son's beautiful face. His wife had wanted to go with him, but for once the barley king stood up to her. "You've done enough," he told her. But he did want his son to go back with him to the castle, where he would have better care. Ari replied that he couldn't leave the capital, because he would soon be starting his classes in the history department. He added that Moli would look after him. Because he knew that his father would repeat his words to his wife, and he would rather have cut out his tongue than admit that Moli had left him. Also, he was convinced that she would soon visit him and that he would be able to win her back. So many other people had come to see him, beginning with the deputy brother of the ER doctor, who said that he was collaborating with the police to find the zealots who had beat him up. There also came an actor and two employees of the department store, as well as the groaner, whose eyes filled with tears when he saw him, and it was Ari who had to do the consoling, repeating that there was no link between the thrashing he received and the incident on the square. Others kept up to date by telephone – his grandmother, the ER doctor, even people he didn't know who sympathized with him. But from Moli, not a word. Not the slightest sign of life. Nothing.

His father got him a room with a television set, and Ari watched every local news report. From them he learned that the anti-zealot demonstrations had proliferated since his beating. The anarchists were organizing them as well, and as usual with extremists, their demonstrations were more sensationalistic than ideological. If there were religious freedom in the country, they said, then they should have the right to choose their own prophets, and their own way to practise their religion. And the prophets they chose were the philosophers of the cynical school of Antiquity, whose cult – the term "cynic" having been derived from the Greek word for "dog" – consisted in living like dogs, free of the rules imposed by society, copulating when they were so inclined, no matter where, without a thought for whoever might be present.

Ari watched all the reports on the demonstrations, read all the articles devoted to them. He saw Moli in none of them, nor any mention of her name. But without a doubt she was still in the city – nothing in the world would have made her give up her courses at the Conservatory. And if she was still in the capital, why was she not taking part in the demonstrations? And above all, why did she not ask how he was, even if it were by telephone?

If, in despair, he had considered retreating, like a hermit, to somewhere deep in the woods, Moli's indifference changed his mind. His only thought now was to get even. And as anger is like fire, becoming fiercer the more it has consumed, he devoted the rest of his stay in the hospital to feeding it.

He only had to cast his mind back to the final days of their togetherness. Moli wanted no more of his caresses, no longer laughed at his jokes. She sought him out all the time, ready to take offence at everything he said, even at his silences, to provoke a quarrel and to justify her departure. She knew exactly what buttons to push to make her lover react, what words would hurt him most. And the more Ari stirred up the dregs of his memories, the more Moli's perfidious words and actions returned to him. The extent of her narcissism, as well. Such as the tendency she had, in the company of her actor friends, to refer everything to herself and to say just about anything as long as she was listened to and was the centre of attention. And her vanity was so exaggerated since she had been admitted to the Conservatory that she had begun to look down on him, laughing at his pathetic job as a stock boy, forgetting that she was dancing naked every night before a pack of deviants and that he had renounced a kingdom for her. That didn't stop her, however, from drawing on that "pathetic" job to concoct for herself an anti-zealot mission and to leap instantly from anonymity to the most outrageous media coverage. He could still see the little flame of triumph dancing in the pupils of her eyes when she talked about the media attention she was receiving. Yes, it was hard to admit, but he could no longer avoid the evidence: His mother the barley queen had got things right. Only an opportunistic tart would seek fame by showing herself naked in front of the cameras. And if Moli were no longer doing it, if, ambitious as she was, she had agreed to shift from media frenzy to total anonymity, it was because her new lover, with more balls and more cash, was readying a move that would put her name in lights. Come to think of it, if she moved in with her ballsy millionaire, she must have already been involved with him when she kept saying that she loved her Ari and would love only him, for as long as the number of days equalled the number of nights. And like an idiot, he stocked the damned shelves to pay the rent while she groped other crotches in order to ferret out the dupe who could attend to all her needs. That thought churned up other images accompanied by sucks and groans that coagulated in his brain like clots of blood. And when the deputy came back to see him and to tell him that he had identified the men who had beaten him and to ask him what punishment he recommended, Ari replied:

"Order them to set fire to the Conservatory."

The deputy shot him the same livid look as the zealot to whom he had suggested that he serve his wife breakfast in bed.

"Are you having me on?" the deputy said.

"Your supporters set fire to the Harem."

"Don't jump to conclusions, my boy. If the masses tend to believe the worst, that is not appropriate to someone of your background and your education. For justice's sake, spend some days with us before judging us."

26

THE DEPUTY LIVED with his wife and their three daughters in a large house guarded by two police officers. The oldest daughter was Ari's age, the others, twins, were two years younger. Like their mother, the three of them were charmed by the beauty and the manners of their young guest, and when their father revealed the source of those bruises, still visible on his face, they begged him to punish the guilty parties.

"You saw how my wife and daughters reacted?" the deputy said when he found himself alone with Ari. "Imagine what they would say if I had had buildings with people in them set on fire. But, you will ask, if it's not my men who burned down Harem, then who? I can only wonder. Our party has the wind in its sails, and our enemies will do anything to tarnish our image, even if all we're doing is spreading God's word. And we must spread it wider, my boy. Otherwise our country is doomed. You only have to see to what extremes some people have taken their perversions in the name of freedom of religion and self-expression. My family, like yours, has always believed in the advancement of our people. And after we've made so much progress, with so many advances, these profligates want to reduce us to the level of dogs. Do you think they're asking themselves whether you can erect a society on that foundation, if in fact they want to build anything at all? No, the public display of those long-winded charlatans has only one goal: to be in the news and to attract attention. Ah, for that they'll do anything. You just have to watch them. They outdo each other with their outrageous outbursts, ridiculing our secular values, passing off their puny vexations as metaphysical anguish. Alas, vanity is not restricted to artists. Everything is now in the image you project, and it is vanity rather than wisdom that rules the world. Fortunately, there are men who, to rescue us from the carnival of the ephemeral, are ready to give their all. The richness of their hearts. The great treasure of their minds. The fortunes they have acquired through the sweat of their brow or inherited from their parents. I hope you will be among their number and that you will help to curb this virus before it infects all of our youth, as it almost infected you and destroyed you. I will not ask for the details – I can easily imagine them. Why else would you have asked me to burn the Conservatory, you who, during our last conversation, swore only by the name of your actress? You say nothing? It will come. Until then, I beg you, do not ruin your life for one misguided moment. You can avenge yourself just as well by being the nemesis of decay and by doing good. I too once loved for a first time in an unreasonable and absolute fashion. I too was set adrift by a betrayal, and in my bewilderment, I allowed myself to be overcome by bitterness. Then I met my wife and understood that there is always a door that opens when another is closed, that every ending can lead to a renewal. Would it not be the same for you? Turn your eyes away for a moment from a door that was closed before you, and ask yourself: might it be that in his infinite wisdom, God has led you to me? That your beating was only designed to prevent you from committing the irreparable, because a greater destiny awaits you? My eldest works at the party's religious centre. Go with her tomorrow, talk to her colleagues. Talk to the director. You will perhaps find there an answer to those questions.

27

ARI HAD ACCEPTED the deputy's invitation for no other reason than to indulge his vengeful wrath. The only fires he had ever in his life lit were bonfires. To reduce the Conservatory to ash, he needed help from those who had set Harem ablaze. The deputy could easily claim that his party was hostile to any form of violence, there were hotheads in every group. Had he not seen one of them throw himself at Moli, threatening to burn her alive, when she pulled off her clothes? He had to find those hotheads and began by looking for them at the religious centre, which he visited the next day with the deputy's eldest daughter.

The centre occupied a five-story building near the main railroad station. The girl wanted to show him around, but Ari preferred to wander through on his own so as to ferret things out freely.

He began in the basement and found himself in a studio for the visual arts. But those who worked there, rather than creating new works, were correcting those of artists who had strayed from God's way, as they described it. More precisely, they were altering, censoring, or masking statues and other human representations, eliminating any detail that might encourage impure thoughts. Ari wanted to tell them that God had created those details so that man and woman would become one flesh, but he had come there to win over the zealots and make them talk, not to provoke them. He only mentioned the three men he'd seen in the cemetery, hoping to learn their names. Like the deputy, they replied that the three guys were surely agitators ordered to sully the reputation of the zealots: At the religious centre, they only corrected works that were brought to them. Ari did not pursue the matter. He went up to the main floor, chatted with the people working there, then on the second floor attended a history lecture delivered with utter disrespect for the truth. Ari didn't protest, he just restricted himself to mentioning, in passing, the Harem fire. He was told that the zealots were against any form of violence, because only those who bring about love and peace would be called children of God. Whatever charms and strategies he tried to use, he was repeated the same rigmarole on the third floor, and he began to despair, when the deputy's daughter came to find him on the fourth floor to tell him that the centre's director wanted to see him.

"He's also the party's spiritual guide and will be best able to answer your questions," she said, leading Ari to his office. "Listen carefully to his answers. It's God who speaks from his mouth."

The man indeed had the aspect of a prophet not given to smiling. But what struck Ari was the portrait of Darwin hung on the wall. What was the picture of the father of the theory of evolution doing in a creationist's office?

His guide saw his astonishment and told him:

"That is your destiny that you see there. At least that was the deputy's intuition. How disappointed he will be when he will learn that despite all that he told you yesterday, you persist in your idiocy."

He held a piece of paper out to Ari.

"Take this. Put it in your pocket."

"What is it?"

"The telephone number of the demon you are seeking. Rather than appreciating all the good we are doing here, you have spent the day talking about the Harem fire. I understand, you are a skeptic, as is proper for an educated man. But from that to treat us as pyromaniacs … We grow and we learn in order to see farther, young man, not to look down on others from on high. Anyway. I don't know if this demon set fire to that horrible nightclub. I've only been told that he earns his keep by doing this kind of work. Call him, since you are so determined to ruin your life. And you will ruin it. Sooner or later it will become known you ordered the fire, and while you rot in prison, another conservatory will be built, and your ex-girlfriend will be laughing at you. You will have only yourself to blame, not fate. He who holds the strings never brings someone into the world to rot in prison."

"And what is my fate, according to you?"

"To rid us of the Conservatory."

"I don't understand."

"Nothing happens for nothing, young man. If God has led you here, it is because we have the same goal. This is hardly a secret: We want to close all performance spaces whose attractions are a debauchery for the mind and distance us from God and his paradise. But we want to close them forever. And without violating any commandment. How are we to achieve this? What connection does the Conservatory have with Darwin? With the help of the Lord, all will become clear on its own when the scales of rancor will fall from your eyes and you will submit to the decrees of Providence."

28

H E'S RIGHT, Ari said to himself as he left the holy
man. If I burn down the Conservatory, it will
be reborn from its ashes. But if they succeed in shut-
ting it down and banning all performances, it's Moli's dream that will go up in smoke. So he took the
guide's advice. To show him that he was submissive
to the decrees of Providence, he attended his lectures
on the creation of the universe, on the best way to
break free from one's body in order to draw closer
to God, and on the danger represented by foreign-
ers who, like the larva of insects lodged in imported
bulbs and wood, entered surreptitiously into the
country to destroy the local ecosystem.

You ought to consult a neurologist, he heard his
mother's voice admonishing him.

The barley queen had many faults, but she was not
a zealot. When, in a travel guide, the magnificence of
a temple or cathedral caught her attention, she saw
there monuments raised up to the genius of men,
rather than to the glory of God. And so, seeing her
eldest, so quick to react to foolhardiness, swallowing

the claptrap of the guide without saying boo, she added: *Your beating must have affected your mind.*

On the other hand, Ari's compliance won him the respect of his new companions, and they invited him to take part in their demonstrations. Ari participated with all the ardour of youth, chanting each slogan as if it were the death knell of the Conservatory. Still he was the only one passersby did not make the target of eggs or of filthy words. When the guide saw this, he decided to put him on the party's posters, this time Ari agreed to pose, to enrage Moli, and his pretty face soon lined the capital's streets, with the caption: *Join the army of God!*

The next day twenty or so girls signed up at the religious centre, all wanting to meet him, and one asked him outright to marry her, because she could no longer bear living with him in sin. According to what she said, Ari visited her in her dreams, naked and lustful. To put an end to these distressing dreams, he advised her to read the guide's writings before going to bed. The next day the girl accused him of having returned, this time to shave her pubis, because, she added as she raised her skirt, he preferred to lick her clean-shaven.

Her pubis was indeed newly shaved. Like that of Moli when she danced.

Remember what your last itch cost you, he heard the barley queen saying. *This time let your mother choose the girl.*

Ari struggled bravely against the temptation of the shaven pubis. Not to please his mother. It was the hour for the TV news, and he wanted to hear what Moli would say about him and his posters. But again, he did not hear the traitress's voice, did not even see in the demonstrations the beautiful face he now hated. He did see, however, the photo of the groaner. According to the host, he had been sodomized with a rolling pin and buried alive.

Ari ran to find the deputy and said to him:

"Don't tell me that this was the work of vile agitators intent on sullying the party's reputation. I'm going back home to use my fortune to find those who buried my friend alive and to have you hanged along with them."

The deputy was not used to being talked to in this way. But rather than throwing Ari out, as he had done during their first encounter, he replied:

"You do not only have the appearance and the charisma of a hero, but also a hero's integrity and loyalty towards friends. You lack only one virtue: patience. And if the scoundrels who killed your friend are hiding among us, I will find them just as I found those who attacked you and I will hang them myself."

"And the Conservatory?"

"Patience, my boy."

"Classes have started."

"If you want to speed things up, ask your parents to contribute to our cause."

"I will not go down on my knees before my mother without even knowing when and how that would close the Conservatory and the theatres."

The deputy dithered, talked of a grandiose project that would lead to important changes. And when Ari urged him to be more specific, he talked of a machine that would put an end to the world's moral disorientation and to the improvised theatre that life had become, to bring humanity to that point in time the saints called Before the Fall.

Ari didn't give a hoot about the world's moral disorientation. He wanted to know how a machine would be able to close the Conservatory, once and for all.

"By sending a man into the past," the deputy replied. "Back to the year 1831, to be exact. To eliminate Darwin before he embarked for the Galapagos islands. Because all our problems derive from the satanic theory of evolution, my boy. The plans are made. We only need the money to construct the machine. And the sooner we can build it, the sooner we will shut down all those sites where every day our sacred values are under attack."

Ari was too disgusted to laugh. Could it be that an intelligent man was committed to a project as far-fetched as a time machine? He couldn't help saying, however, this time with a touch of irony:

"And is the killing of a man not a threat to our sacred values?"

"How could it be if Darwin were dead and buried for a century?"

"He was not dead in1831."

"And if we do not eliminate him, would he still be alive?"

"No, but we would be killing all his descendants."

"How could you kill children who were not yet conceived? And even if you did away with his entire line, the Lord, with the flood, did he not drown all human sinners, sparing only Noah and his family?"

Ari had read a lot about fanaticism, but this was the first time that he had seen it dumb everything down and render futile any discussion.

"You're right," he said, anxious to get away. "Rather than defending the dead, let us save the living."

"You are truly the son that I always wanted to have," the deputy said, embracing him. "Run to call your parents, and your name will be inscribed for all time in the history books of which you are so fond."

29

A RI DID PHONE HIS FATHER, but only to tell him
that he had decided to return to the kingdom.
However, he first had to settle a debt. And when his
father sent him the money he had asked for, he called
the "demon" whose phone number the guide had
given him.

The Conservatory burned two days later. In the
middle of the night, as Ari demanded, so there would
be no victims.

The zealots were suspected, and the zealots in turn
accused their enemies of having burned down this
school of debauchery in order once more to discredit
them. Only their spiritual guide suspected Ari. But
he shared his suspicions with nobody. Instead he delivered an inflammatory speech to unleash the passions of his flock. To absolve themselves of their past
crimes, his flock would react most cruelly to the false
accusations, there would be deaths, and with a bit of
luck, a civil war. Being the most violent, the zealots
would take power and impose their ideology.

Of course, Ari also rejoiced at the burning of the Conservatory. He even delayed his departure from the capital to see Moli's expression in front of the cameras when she would talk about her dreams that had gone up in smoke. He would then take the reins of the barley kingdom to use his power and his fortune, to block any attempt on the part of the traitress to make a career as an actress.

And in fact, he saw Moli on television the day after the fire. But only in a photo. Along with the photos of two other students who, having worked late at the Conservatory, had decided to spend the night there.

Ari's first reaction was to change the channel to find one that contradicted this news. But no matter how he punched and zapped, every station displayed the same photos, repeated the same names.

What is this curse that pursues me wherever I go? he said to himself. *Yes, I hoped that bad things would happen to her. So that she would suffer the way she made me suffer. Ah! Why didn't I escape into the deep woods? Would it not have been better to shut myself off behind those trees with my anger rather than cause the deaths of three people?*

He was still bemoaning his unhappy fate when the telephone in the suite started to ring. It was the luxury suite where his parents stayed when they came to the capital. His father had offered it to him, and no one else knew where he was to be found, save the barley queen. But Ari was in no condition to talk, especially to his mother. And as the ringing went on proclaiming that she knew he was there, and the reception desk confirmed it, he went out so he would stop hearing it.

The capital was in turmoil. Riots had broken out, and rumours were making the rounds, proclaiming that buses were bringing in hundreds of zealots from the countryside. *What have I done*, Ari thought. *I have not only set fire to the Conservatory, but to the whole country!*

A moment later, he added: *It's all her fault. If she hadn't stripped down on the square, the groaner wouldn't have fired me, they wouldn't have set fire to Harem, and we would be working and studying now as we had planned. But she couldn't wait to finish at the Conservatory before getting on television. And her vanity not only cost us our jobs, but the groaner paid with his life. All I wanted was to burn the Conservatory. If she was inside, it's because God had kept her there to punish her for the death of the groaner and the other disasters she had caused. As the guide said, nothing is accidental.*

"Don't look down, my friend!" a beggar shouted at him, seeing him pass by, bent under the weight of his thoughts. "You know what's awaiting us down there!"

Ari was so obsessed with blaming everything on Moli that he heard nothing. Not even the thunder rumbling in the distance. Nor, closer by, the girl who was calling out to him.

It was Melody. She was going to demonstrate with her friends against the burning of the Conservatory, and when she spotted Ari, she ran to him and said:

"I lied to you. It's Moli who asked me to tell you that she no longer loved you. Now that she's dead, I can tell you. Moli didn't leave you for someone else. There was no other man. It's your mother who forced her to break up with you. Not in person; she sent someone to see her. He didn't give his name, or who he represented. Moli was sure it was your mother who sent him. He came to see her just a day after the Harem fire, and she concluded that your mother had had it destroyed so that she'd lose her job and bend more easily to her will. In short, the guy insisted that Moli choose between you or her career. If she chose her career, they would be covering all her expenses during her years of study. Don't blame her for having chosen her career. She had been dreaming of it since she was very little. In any case, if she had chosen you, the guy would have had her expelled from the Conservatory. He had even threatened to disfigure her with acid if she said a word. I'm glad I can finally tell you the truth. Moli doesn't deserve your hatred. I hope you won't hate me either for having made you suffer with my lie. I lied to you to protect Moli."

That's what Melody had to say to him, and when she had done so, she left to rejoin her friends.

Ari stayed frozen there, while the lightning and thunder intensified. And when the storm broke over the city, rather than run for shelter, he raised his head towards the sky, as if praying for the lightning to strike him.

119

30

◆

As a child, Ari had drawn his mother as a princess and positioned a sun above her head. Although the sun is often present in children's drawings, in the barley queen's eyes this one was unique, and represented her beloved prince. And so she'd had it framed and hung it in her bedroom, and since the departure of her eldest she looked at it every night, eyes filled with tears. Tears that turned to smiles when her husband told her that her offspring was returning to the fold. She ordered the castle's windows opened to freshen the air, flowers arranged in vases, and the best caterer engaged for the banquet she would give in honour of the prodigal son. Finally, she replaced all the photos on her dressing table with more recent ones, depositing a kiss on each one before slipping it into its frame.

"Why did he decide to come back?" her mother asked, when she heard about Ari's return.

"Because his tramp ditched him."

"They adored each other. What did you do, you wretch, to separate them?"

"I prayed, and God answered my prayers."

"Be careful, my daughter. *Thou shalt not take God's name in vain; because the Eternal leaves not unpunished one who uses his name to deceive.*"

Not being pious, the barley queen cared nothing for the heavens and only quoted the holy books so as to manipulate and obtain what she desired. And so she burst out laughing when her mother came at her like a preacher spitting hellfire and damnation. And when she'd stopped laughing, she said:

"Reread your holy books, mama. You'll see that your God would actually be proud of me. Because only a being as hard and intransigent as he is can work for the good of all."

There is no limit to self-justification, and at this game, to paraphrase Ari, no one is as daunting as one who never has any doubts. And not even the shadow of a doubt concerning herself ever entered the mind of the barley queen when she learned an hour later what her younger child had done.

When he learned that his brother was coming home, Junior had thought again of the care his aunt devoted to her paraplegic son. So that no one would see him and prevent him from maiming himself, as Ari had done in the cemetery, he had jumped from his bedroom window, feet first, in the hope that the shock on landing would break his legs. But he only succeeded in blowing out a knee. And if he thought that his mother would take pity on his fate, learning that he would limp for the rest of his life, he soon learned better when she entered his hospital room, calling him an idiot and a millstone around her neck, adding – and that was what caused him the greatest pain – that fortunately she had another son to console her.

The barley queen only became less smug – and this just for appearance's sake – when she learned of Moli's death. She smothered Moli's mother with affection, mingled her tears with her own, even offered her a private helicopter to transport her to the capital to retrieve her daughter's remains. Not being informed of what the barley queen had done to her only child – Moli had spoken about it only to Melody – her mother kissed her employer's hands, so touched was she by her compassion and generosity.

Like Moli's mother and half the country, the barley queen suspected the zealots of having set fire to the Conservatory. And that night, she thanked them in her thoughts, because they had just chased off the little cloud that had inserted itself between the sun and the princess in her son's drawing. As long as she was alive, Moli could have one day told Ari everything. How would he have reacted? The barley queen dared not even imagine it. *Pity she didn't kick the bucket sooner and spare me all these troubles*, she thought, just as her mother called her to say:

"Congratulations!"

Was she accusing her of Moli's death, or had she at last understood that the Eternal was on her side?

"For what exactly?" the barley queen asked before reacting.

"You haven't heard? It was on the television news."

"What was on the television news?"

"Ari. He was arrested for the Conservatory fire."

31

H E HAD TURNED HIMSELF IN. The investigators, see-ing that the fire was clearly the work of a pro-fessional, wanted to know how he had proceeded. So as not to reveal his ignorance, Ari only opened his mouth to repeat that he had acted alone to avenge an acting student who'd ditched him. The investigators knew plenty of tricks to get the truth out of him, but they dared not use them on the son of the barley king. Plus, the conservative government, in order to absolve the zealots, told them to go along with his confessions in order to lock him up.

Ari refused the services of a lawyer. The barley king had hired the best criminal lawyer in the land, who was quick to find arguments to exonerate his client of the crime he claimed to have committed. His most powerful argument involved the testimony of the grand hotel employees. All swore that Ari had spent the night of the fire in his parents' suite.

"They're lying," the accused declared to his lawyer. "Because my father is one of the hotel's best clients. And if you use their false testimony, I'll say that I also poisoned the old hermit who gave me shelter in the forest." This he added in the hope that there was an afterlife and that Moli was seeing and hearing all he did and said in order to be condemned and to expiate his crime.

His parents could, however, see and hear perfectly well, and when the lawyer repeated his words to them, they asked for a meeting in order to reason with him.

Ari wanted to talk only to his father.

When she learned that, his mother sent him a message. It said:

I do not believe that you have abandoned God to the point of refusing to devote ten minutes to the woman who gave you life and who has aided you, devoted and vigilant, since your first cry, expecting nothing in return, not even a modest breakfast in bed. You owe me an audience, if only in exchange for the twelve hours of labour you had me endure in giving you birth.

Ari did not reply, remaining firm in his resolution to speak only to his father, one on one, to inform him of the duplicity, the egoism, and the nastiness of his mother.

Well aware of the bond between her elder son and his grandmother, the barley queen asked her to intervene.

And so the old woman called Ari in prison and said:

"Do not make me regret my behaviour, dear heart. I helped you because you wanted to find your own way, not to spend your life in prison with fools whose only thought is to break your head or your arse."

"I killed three people. It's what I deserve."

"Don't be stupid. You don't even know how to light a fire in a fireplace."

"I did it, grandma. And it's not my dreams that are responsible for my misfortune, but those of your daughter."

"It's not her fault all the same, if Moli ditched you."

"My father will tell you what really happened. That's if his wife will allow him to come and see me alone."

32

HIS GRANDMOTHER WAS RIGHT, the prisoners were for the most part hardened criminals who spent their days pumping iron or scratching their crotches. The barley king and queen knew it and they had used their connections to obtain a cell on a private wing for their offspring, a cell that had been occupied only once, by a prisoner who had left behind on the walls this riddle: *What is it that turns in circles but goes constantly forward?* And it was in the intimacy of this cell, rather than in the visiting room, that Ari talked to his father, one on one, as he had demanded.

The barley king had lost weight and his wrinkles seemed to reflect the sorrows of their two lives. Ari knew that what he was going to tell him would tear him apart, and it was with a heavy heart that he told his father what Melody had said.

The barley king replied:

"Since you left us, your mother has only once intervened in your life, when she came to see you in the capital. She swore that to me. On the lives of her children. Why should I believe a stranger? Nothing is more sacred to a mother, Ari, than the lives of her children."

"I thought so too. And I told myself that they must have been mad, when, in my history books, I read that queens had poisoned their sons to keep their throne, because I could not believe that a sane mother could kill the flesh of her flesh. I now know that certain mothers are capable of anything."

"Get these horrid suspicions out of your head, my son. If you cannot admit that Moli left you for another, do not pour out your rage onto your mother. She adores you."

"As long as I do whatever she wants."

"I admit it, she's a bit of a mother hen …"

Ari became angry despite himself.

"Mother hen? She's a tyrant. Just think of the way she treats you when you resist her, what she says to you and makes you suffer till you buckle under."

"Maybe she's a bit authoritarian, stubborn and angry, but it's always in the interests of the family and the kingdom."

"What is this power she has over you? Why are the good so meek and the heartless so powerful, papa? Because I did not give in to all her desires, she destroyed all my hopes, my life. And she's the one you're defending?"

"What do you want me to do?" the barley king cried out in his turn. "She is so certain that she alone is in the right and always just, that sometimes I want to strangle her. Is that what you want? For me to strangle her? The mother of my children? The woman who for twenty years has shared my dreams, my cares, my joys? The companion who, with her assertive manner has made me the barley king and tripled the fortune that you and your brother will inherit?"

"I will inherit nothing, papa. Because I did not let myself to be led by the nose, I'll have to spend the rest of my life in this cell."

"No, cooperate with your lawyer, and you could be out of here tomorrow."

"And let my mother win again?"

His father shook his head.

"She's right, you're like her."

"I know. I realized that when Melody told me what my mother had done to Moli. I thought that she had no more power over me but I discovered that I was just as vengeful as she is. But I can admit to my faults and my errors. I'm going to assume them and serve the sentence that I have coming to me."

"Then my sorrow is complete. And I don't even know what I've done to deserve it. I've been a good son and a faithful husband. What I inherited, I spent my life making it flourish, just as my father did with what his father left to him. I always treated my employees fairly. They all loved me and blessed me. The whole country envied me. As much for the success of my agricultural land as for the beauty and intelligence of my wife and those two heirs she gave me. All that was left, to make me happy, was to see them as fathers as well. But I will not have this ultimate reward for my labours. One wants to have himself condemned for life, and the other wants to take his own life."

"Junior?"

"He threw himself from his bedroom window."

"When?"

"The day you said you were coming home. He only injured his knee. But the next time …"

She also ruined the life of her youngest, and I probably feel guiltier than she does, Ari thought, while his father grasped his hands, kissed them, and said:

"Let the lawyer get you out of here, my boy. I too gave you life. Do it for me, for all the hopes I placed in you, for all the workers who will lose their jobs, for all the children who'll starve to death. I won't have the heart to lead the kingdom if I have no more heirs. I beg you. Forget your anger, call on all the best you inherited from me, and save our family, our kingdom, our line."

Though he was overwhelmed with pity by his father's suffering, Ari could not help crying out:

"How can you ask me to forget the deaths I caused, you who instilled in me the sense of justice and responsibility? Would you have forgotten them, in my place?"

"I would not have set fire to the Conservatory."

You're avoiding the question, Ari wanted to answer, but a huge noise, a din straight from hell, prevented him.

33

T HE PRISONERS' LIVES were ones of repetition and monotony. To let off steam, they trounced one another. The pretext wasn't important. Someone walked on your shadow and you threw yourself at his throat like a buoy tossed to a castaway drifting on a sea of boredom. But they rarely went after the guards, even if they hated them as much as the guards held them in contempt. First of all, the screws were armed and more brutal, and when you greased their palms, they got you something that for a while allowed you to forget the bleakness of your daily life. And so a few weeks earlier, two screws brought in the statue of a naked woman that the zealots had not yet destroyed. They installed it in a storeroom and, for a price, a prisoner could spend ten minutes with her. The statue was such a success that the screws doubled the cost of admission. Unfortunately, they did it on the day the barley king was visiting his son, and the noise they heard was the furor of the prisoners, who, out of control, disarmed the two guards and cured them of their greed with a bullet.

The riot that ensued was terrible and bloody, with the mutineers attacking both the guards and the rival gangs among the prisoners. If the latter only had makeshift knives to defend themselves, they were infused with the same rage, and when they got hold of a rival, they beheaded him, then lined up the heads like a row of onions, on the line separating the two camps.

Overwhelmed by what was going on, the warden called in the army. A battalion surrounded the prison, but dared not go inside; the mutineers had taken three guards hostage, and threatened to chop them down like trees if they were attacked. The commander knew they weren't bluffing: When a mob is on a rampage, there is no logical or rational behaviour. Moreover, the barley queen threatened to strip him of his position if anything happened to her son and her husband. Not knowing that the latter had suffered a cardiac arrest when, in addition to his emotions experienced with his son, he had learned from the guard what the mutineers had done. Unfortunately for him, they had also occupied the passage leading to the main building. If the guard opened the gate to the private wing to seek help, the mutineers would kill everyone in it.

The hours that followed were terrible for the barley king and his son. Seeing his father die before his eyes, Ari wondered what he could do to help him. His breathing weak and irregular, the barley king listened to him with the fixed gaze of someone who no longer was able to speak. Persuaded that this eye contact could keep his father alive, Ari talked to him non-stop, sometimes stroking his head, offering him words of love and encouragement, sometimes recalling memories of an earlier time, carefree and happy, and of the enormous mark that his father had left.

"Not only did you teach me the precepts of justice, honour, and loyalty, you also piqued my interest in the past by talking to me about barley, the oldest cultivated cereal, without which we might not have had the Hanging Gardens of Babylon, the pyramids, and the Acropolis. And in the evening, seeing me surfing the Web to learn all about these wonders and the men who built them, you said – do you remember? – you said: 'So, son, what's new in history?'"

He hoped for a smile, at least. Instead he saw the exact moment when the light went out.

He spent three days with the corpse of the man who had given him life.

Why did I not respond to his call, that night, by the train tracks? he asked himself. I would have renounced my dreams, to take the road traced by my mother, consisting of obedience and regret, but my father would still be alive. Moli, too.

When the cell began to smell of decomposition, he thought he would go mad. Not only because the stench was unbearable, but because it was that of his father, the man he loved most in the world. And he could not flee, as he had done with the old hermit. He could turn away his eyes or close them, but he could not stop breathing.

34

THE MUTINEERS HELD the three guards hostage so as to swap them for their own freedom. When their demands were rejected, they put the prison to the torch. The battalion commander then gave his troops the order to attack, and, in the massacre that followed, the soldiers found Ari huddled in the corner of his cell. They took him to the exit where, fearing that he would be locked up with his ghosts in another prison, he took advantage of the confusion to slip away.

Avoiding the roads and towns, where his prisoner's attire would have betrayed him to the authorities, he walked through fields, addressing his grandmother in his thoughts.

I ought to have shut myself off in the old hermit's forest when I had only a heartbreak to contend with, he said to her. *Too many sorrows have befallen me since then for me to want to get up every morning and busy myself with beekeeping and gardening. Please, don't tell me that my misfortunes must have a silver lining. Even your daughter wouldn't dare claim that. Ah, why did she ever bring me into the world? People like her should never have children. Look at what I inherited, determining my fate, even before I had a chance to plot it out for myself ... It's so unfair, grandma. That a few genes from a parent could determine your destiny forever after. All I wanted was to live my life. And cursed fate when reality did not conform to my expectations. Others wanted me to believe that everything was God's will, the decree of fate, or the fruit of chance. Was it God or fate that prevented me from apologizing to the zealot who was shopping with his wife for a tray? I wouldn't have lost my job, the groaner would still be alive, Moli and her friends too, and papa would not have come to visit me in prison. But I didn't want to apologize. The cursèd character inherited from your daughter prevented me from doing so. How to escape from that, grandma? I thought that walled up in a cell, I would atone for my crimes and would not hurt anyone else. But all those walls and bars didn't stop me from acting again like her. My father wanted to come the day before the mutiny. I refused to see him, because she would have come with him, and I didn't want to let her win. Thus I killed the gentlest, the most righteous and generous man I knew, and reduced all the memories of him to this stench that pursues me, even here, in the open air.*

That is what Ari said to his grandma as he crossed the fields. And when, covered in dust and wretchedness, he found himself on the bank of a river, he saw nothing fortuitous there, only his grandma's response to his ramblings.

The water was perfectly dark, deep, and rapid for someone seeking to put an end to his future and his share of remorse and complaints. But he was a good swimmer, and to give the waters the greatest advantage, he explored the river, looking for eddies, or a bridge or a cliff high enough for his plunge, to knock him unconscious when he hit the surface. And when he finally found it, his last thought was for his mother: She would never know that he had killed himself if his body were not found. *She will have still lost me forever, I will have gained that at least*, he answered himself. And instantly regretted that thought: *I'm thinking like her, even when it comes to my death! For sure, alive, I could no more free myself from this defect than shift my palm lines, as grandma would say.*

Before leaping, he wanted to look one last time at the sun that he loved so dearly. "Farewell sun," he said. "Farewell, dreams and plans and all the beautiful things that my spite has robbed me of," he added, when, as in one of those coincidences so widespread in life, but that one dares not include in a fiction for fear that the story would seem too contrived, he heard voices crying for help.

35

SOME PEOPLE WERE STANDING on the bank, upstream from Ari, while others were running towards him, shouting that a child had fallen into the water and none of them knew how to swim. And in fact, when Ari looked at the river, he saw a young boy being carried away by the current. Forgetting his troubles, he dove in and, swimming so hard his arms and his lungs ached, he caught the youngster and brought him to shore.

"How can we express our gratitude?" the boy's father, a sturdy, balding man with densely tattooed muscles, said. "Tell me and you'll have it."

Ari's only thought was to get away.

"You won't go far with your convict's clothing," the man said. "Many prisoners have escaped, and the soldiers are combing the region to find them. You'll leave when they've stopped searching. You risked your life to save my son. I am your friend, in life and in death."

The long trek across the fields, and the rescue of the child, had so exhausted Ari that he didn't protest.

He let himself be led into a house where he stripped off his wet clothes and dried himself, thinking that not only had he inherited his mother's defects, but that he'd also been born unlucky. Why would he chance upon a drowning child, just as he was going to put an end to his suffering? He would have been at peace by now. And maybe with his father, and with Moli too.

And so, rather than rejoicing at having saved a child's life and enjoying his status as a hero, he spent the evening cursing his misfortune, as, in dry clothes, he joined his hosts, gathered together in the garden, to celebrate him and to honour him. He did learn that the bald man was their leader, that they lived communally, and applied themselves to the cultivation and sale of cannabis, their plantings covering more than two hundred hectares, that they supplied the prison guards with marijuana and other drugs that, in turn, the guards sold to the prisoners, along with other articles as well, such as the sculpture that had provoked the prison's burning and killing. But rather than boasting about all that, these strapping, ribald outlaws talked only of Ari's dive, without ever asking him why he was in prison, as if the fact of having risked his life to save a child was the only thing about him that mattered. And when Ari had had enough food and drink, the bald man said to him:

"I had three sons. The second one drowned, three years ago. Had you not dived into the river, I would have lost the youngest as well. So do me a favour, let me do something for you."

"I have everything I need. Really. All is well."

"No, all cannot be well. The lowlifes, the deviants, and the crooks, I can smell them a mile away. You're not one of them. And yet you were in prison. Do you have an enemy who wrongfully accused you? You can tell me. I'll take care of him, and you'll have nothing more to fear from him."

"No one wrongfully accused me."

"Is there someone who gave you a hard time in prison? Because if someone gave you a hard time there, you should tell me."

"No one gave me a hard time in prison."

"That's hard to believe. A good-looking boy like you ..."

He seemed disappointed. Ari could repeat that no one harassed him in prison, that he was owed nothing, that he had dived into the river because he couldn't let a child drown: to no avail. The bald man felt that he owed him something, and he wanted to pay his debt. To please him, Ari finally told him that he needed a bit of money and an identity card.

"You will have them," the other replied, smiling once more. "My telephone number as well, to contact me if in future someone decides to bother you or to interfere with your desires and your plans. Meanwhile, if you want a woman ..."

"No thank you."

"After all this time locked up ..."

"I'm too tired," said Ari, to end the discussion, knowing that he would need neither money nor a new identity, to face up to what awaited him.

36

ALL HE HAD TO DO was to regain the resolve that had inhabited him when he first approached the river. But when he wakened the next morning, as he was reviewing the reasons why he had to end his days, the bald man's spouse, whom everyone called Carom because she beat all the men at billiards, brought him breakfast and asked him to stay for another day.

"As big and strong as they are," she said, "our men are scared to death of the water and none of them has learned to swim. I've already lost a child in that river. I beg you, teach my youngest how to swim. Boys of that age are careless, and he's bound to fall into the water again, like the one I lost."

The memory of the son who now lay in the river's deeps swelled her eyelids with tears, and Ari, although anxious to free himself from his sins, spent the day teaching the boy to swim.

"I will bless you to the end of my days," Carom said when he finally came out of the water.

The country had no sea and no lake, and only the rich with swimming pools knew how to swim. And so Ari had barely dried himself off when other mothers begged him to teach their young ones to swim before fear of the water overwhelmed them. Ari wondered what his father would have done in his place – his mother, he knew, would never have put the wishes of others before her own – and he decided to cling to life for a few more days. And the night of his last swimming lesson, while the mothers set up in the garden a long table to thank him, while he was still convinced that only death could conciliate his soul, he told himself that his short life would not have been a total disaster: He would have taught children to swim and saved a few lives.

But a banal incident once again undermined all his plans, when the clan's righthand man, a gorilla who might have scared you to death just by squinting his eyes, arrived, pushing ahead of him the bald man's eldest son, a lanky and lumbering adolescent. Instantly, the mothers circling Ari to ensure that he had everything he needed, rose, eyes turned towards the head of the table where the bald man was enthroned.

The boy had been missing for five days, and the gorilla told the bald man that he had been found in the company of a girl belonging to a rival clan. The bald man thanked the man with a wave of his hand, then poured his son a drink. That did nothing to lighten the mood, no one went back to eating or drinking, no one made a sound. Except for the bald man, who, seeing his son dip his lips into the wine, said to him:

"Drink up, big guy. If you're able to mount a lady, you should be able to swallow your drink in one shot."

The boy took a mouthful and almost choked.

"Swallow it all, you'll feel better," the bald man said.

With a trembling hand, the youngster raised his glass again, emptied it, then put it back down on the table.

"I said, swallow it all."

"It's empty."

"Swallow your glass," his father said.

"There's nothing left. Look. How can I swallow an empty glass?"

"Piece by piece, chewing each one thoroughly."

The boy ventured a weak smile, as if his father were making a joke. But his father did not return the smile. He said:

"Judas. I've fed you for eighteen years. I've told you all my secrets and dreams. And you betray me for a slut? And yet I'd warned you. I told you what we do to those who break our clan's rules. And the punishment awaiting those who violate its sanctity. The reasons why your slut's father let you screw her. Did I not tell you, yes or no, that she'd let you fiddle with her muff just so you'd tell her our secrets?"

"That's not true! She loves me!"

"So now we're putting love on the scale. Like your mother. Sentimental. And hopeless. Swallow your glass, boy. Otherwise, on the soul of your dead brother, I will force it down your throat myself, piece by piece."

And he would be capable of doing it. Ari only had to witness the furor with which he broke the glass, while the gorilla was gluing the boy to his chair with his tree trunk arms. So he said:

"That's enough! Siring and feeding a child does not give you the right to govern his heart as well!"

It would not have been worse if Ari had spat in the bald man's face.

37

T HE CLAN WAS GOVERNED by strict rules and all its members had to observe them to the letter. Ari knew it, but he could not hold his tongue while a teenage boy was being force-fed shards of glass because he'd fallen for a girl his father disapproved of. Besides, not being a member of the clan, he could contest the rules, especially since the bald man had promised to give him whatever he desired. And so he asked permission to speak, and the bald man, bound by his promise, had to contain his anger and grant it to him.

Ari said to him:

"Last week, you rejoiced that your youngest son had escaped death. Today you want to kill your eldest because he followed his heart. If you see logic in all that, I see only vanity. Because if it were only a matter of your clan's security, you would have found another way to settle this matter, without putting your child to death."

To support his argument, Ari cited the example of dictators who had sent their sons to be killed on the battlefield. The reasoning was that, if they had sacrificed their own children for the country, the people could only consent when they were called upon to provide more cannon fodder. Alas, only later was it understood that all those sons had not been sacrificed for their native land, but for the greater glory of the supreme leader. And it was for this very reason that the barley queen, his mother, had wanted to sacrifice him, Ari went on, revealing his pedigree to his hosts for the first time, telling them that he'd been born a prince, that he was considered the most favoured son until the day he fell in love with a girl of whom his mother disapproved. The worst, he went on, came about when his mother had forced his sweetheart to leave him, and the vile nature he'd inherited drove him to take such revenge that on the day he had saved the bald man's young son from drowning, he was only approaching the river in order to drown himself. That's where vanity gets you, he said to the bald man, citing, to overcome his resistance, great men such as Gandhi, who said that the most important battle to win was to vanquish one's own demons.

"If you want to serve the interests of your clan," he concluded, "rather than having him swallow shards of glass, tell your son to invite his girlfriend to come here to live, where you can keep an eye on her. If she's not opening her legs just to elicit his secrets, she will do so. If she refuses, I think your son will agree quite willingly never to see her again."

The boy agreed to the proposal, the bald man too, while the women, for whom there was nothing more beautiful and moving than the story of an impossible love, felt drawn to Ari to console him for Moli's loss. But his story had a very different impact on the men. Seeing how he had since his arrival shunned all the girls who trailed after him, they had concluded that he was gay. Now they said:

"What a man! To set fire to a building and burn three people to death to avenge his honour! He must have balls of steel!"

Rather than reminding them that Ari regretted what he had done, Carom wondered how she could prevent the boy who had saved the lives of two of her sons from attempting to absolve his sins in the river.

38

♦

THE BARLEY KING WAS much loved, and a great sadness had come over his kingdom since the announcement of his death. All were now aware of Ari's involvement in the Conservatory fire. Those who knew him could hardly believe that a boy as gentle and caring could do such a thing. When they learned that his father had died while visiting the prison, their shock mutated into a profound sense of injustice. Like Moli's mother, who had closeted herself in her house and covered the windows with a black sheet, they told themselves that, if one of Ari's parents was to pay with their life for the son's crime, fate had chosen the wrong one, reinforcing their conviction that blackguards are favoured by destiny. However, unlike Moli's mother, they continued to work for the barley queen and, when they ran into her, they offered their sympathies with a great sigh.

The barley queen saw through those condolences. Rather than irritating her, they confirmed her in the conviction that the plebs might bleat in private, but they would always live in a state of servitude and hypocrisy. Ah, if only she could talk to her prince, to complete his education and make of him a great leader. But her prince had disappeared. And his disappearance pained her much more than that of her husband. Sick as he was, she knew that his heart would not beat for much longer. The thought that the heart that had beat so near her own was repudiating her was, on the other hand, unbearable. And so she hired private detectives to find him, and also asked her mother to help her, holding her responsible for all the calamities that had befallen the family since she had given her grandson the money for a train to rejoin his whore. And when the old lady sent her on her way, saying that she preferred to communicate directly with her conscience without her daughter's intercession, the daughter ordered the detectives to tap her telephone in case her prince, who adored his grandma, were to call her.

The barley queen asked her mother to locate her prince because she also possessed the gift of divination. If she told Ari that this was all fake, when he had asked her to help him find Moli, it was so that he'd give up on magic thinking and learn to get by on his own. In truth, by concentrating on a name or a face, she was sometimes able to see from a distance what the individual was regarding at that moment, and to deduce the area where he could be found. And she had been doing that constantly since her adored grandson had escaped, to trace him before he could do something irreparable while trying to inflict on his mother some ultimate pain. But every time she concentrated her attention on his beautiful face, all she saw was water.

"Oh, my dear heart," she said, "why are you staring so intently at that water? What dark designs do you envision doing? Turn your eyes away, dear heart, and send me a hopeful sign. Please, remove your eyes from the waves, and direct them at something else. I'll need more information if I am to find you and come to your rescue."

As in response to her wish, the telephone rang. The call was from Carom, who told the old woman how Ari had ended up with her clan, and what he intended to do on leaving it.

"I called my brother – he deals with clan matters in the barley kingdom – and he told me that you alone would be able to persuade the poor boy to renounce his dark plans."

The old woman replied that she was leaving immediately, and begged Carom not to let her grandson out of her sight until she arrived.

39

CAROM STAYED CLOSE to Ari all evening, and when he returned to his room, she stood by his door and only left when her husband told her to go and console her eldest son. He had asked his sweetheart to move in with him, she had refused, and he was sobbing like an infant. Carom was only gone for a few minutes. But when, at dawn, she wanted to tell Ari that his grandma had arrived, she found the room empty, and fainted, thinking that he had gone to join his father and his beloved.

Ari had not gone to join his father and his beloved. He was still sleeping, but forty kilometres from his room, at the foot of the mountain where, according to legend, an eagle had set down, still a babe in arms, the ancestor of his people. For as soon as Carom's call had been intercepted by the barley queen's detectives, she telephoned the bald man to warn him that she was coming to get her son, and that if he made any trouble, she would come down on him with a battalion. And in discovering the cannabis plantation, she added, the soldiers, who were for the most part zealots, would put to the torch not just his plants, but his house as well.

Cornered, the bald man replied:

"If I give him up to you here, it's my wife who will char me like a roast. I'll meet you at the Ancestor's Grotto parking lot. No one's there at night."

And so he lured Carom away from Ari's door, entered the room with his right hand man and a flask of chloroform, and an hour later deposited the barley queen's son at the agreed-upon location. The night was dark, and the site deserted, and as he was wearing only his boxer shorts, Ari thought he was dreaming when he opened his eyes and saw his unfortunate father's helicopter descending from the sky. *I'm going to see him again, talk to him again*, he thought. Then he saw the barley queen emerging from the metal bird and coming towards him, and his joy turned into rage at the thought that the bald man, who had sworn to be his friend, in life and in death, had sold him out as soon as he learned that he was the son of one of the richest women in the land.

"I couldn't wait to tell you," the barley queen said as she approached him. "I've had your sentence commuted with a fine for involuntary homicide. You're a free man," she added, pulling a travel blanket over his shoulders.

"Don't touch me!"

"You'll catch cold."

"It's you who is freezing my blood."

The barley queen's eyes clouded.

"Do you enjoy lacerating the only heart that is yours forever, unconditionally?"

"What about my heart? Did you ever think of that? All it needed to feel good was to breathe in the scent of your perfume. Even in Moli's arms, it pained me to think of your sorrow, and I prayed to God that you would bless our union, that I could at last fully embrace my happiness. I never had that chance. The heart that claimed to love me unconditionally could not be satisfied with my affection. It also demanded utter obedience and devotion."

"I was defending your interests, my treasure. And the facts proved me right. She left you in the lurch as soon as she found someone better."

"She left me because you threatened to disfigure her!"

"The hypocritical, lying monster! No wonder she chose the theatre!"

"It wasn't she who told me, it was her friend."

"Another professional liar, I assume?"

"Just this once, confess to your crimes."

"What crimes? Loving my child? Wanting what's best for him? Wanting to protect him?"

"Because of you, I killed four people!"

"Everyone makes mistakes, my love. You're without salvation only if you persist in your misdoing."

"And what are you doing, then?

"I'm basking in the voice of my beloved son, and the joy that his beautiful face brings me."

"A true snake."

"Abuse me as much as you wish, if it makes you feel better. A mother's back is wider than the earth. And all this poor one asks in return is to grow old beside her child."

"Get that out of your head. I will never reign over the kingdom of a father I killed, under the thumb of a mother I hate."

"Be careful, son. It's better to have all the world's hatred against you than the bitterness of a mother."

"I won't have it for long. And death compared to what I am feeling would be a blessing."

"Then you had better kill me as well. Without you, the world is all darkness."

"You'll get over it. You'll flog yourself for a day or two with an asparagus, and then you'll recover. Because however much you boast about your great mothering heart, you don't have one."

And with these words, he stalked away, as his mother cried:

"No! Ari! My love! Stop, in God's name!"

The two detectives who had accompanied her and who had been ordered to stay in the helicopter leapt to the ground to catch her son. But he had disappeared into the night, pursued by his mother's voice, saying:

"I hope there is a hell and that she is burning in it, the cursèd woman who robbed me of my son, led my husband to his death, and destroyed my house! Ah, mama, why did you give him money for that train?"

40

PURSUED BY HIS MOTHER'S SOBS, echoed by the mountain of the Ancestor, Ari cursed those who had brought him there, after all he had done for the clan.

Do you understand now why I removed myself from the world? he heard the old hermit say. *My cabin is not far. You'll find clothing there, and my bees will give you nothing but honey.*

Ari couldn't care less about the bees and their damn honey. Although he had sworn never to give in to the vindictiveness he'd inherited from his mother, he only thought of getting even with the bald man and his clan. And with a bit of luck, get himself killed while making them pay for their betrayal. But first he had to find some clothes. He searched for them as soon as the sun came up, finding only scarecrows, and when he got close to them in order to strip them of their rags, he heard cries and fled, carving up his feet on the stones. And it was with his bloodied soles that he came to the outskirts of the ER doctor's town. Not daring to show himself in his shorts, he waited for nightfall, plotting his revenge and punishments that were more and more extreme.

"Thank god it's the hour for the soap operas!" the ER doctor said when, seeing him naked in front of her door, she remembered her neighbours' viperish eyes.

She tended to his feet, gave him clothes and shoes, even served him food. Ari was in no mood to frolic and intended to leave as soon as he'd finished eating. In fact, since Moli's death, the very thought of directing his gaze at a girl was for him an insult to the memory of his beloved. And when a succubus offered herself to him – and since he'd decided to end his life, as a sign of protest, his body sent him one every night – on waking, he apologized for this moment of abandon, as if he were committing an act of treason. And so he only agreed to spend the night at the ER doctor's when she informed him that she was dead tired, to the point that she had not even taken care of her parakeets.

"I've had a hard day. It began with three children falling into a river. I was only able to revive one of them …"

When she awoke the next day, Ari was gone, leaving a two-word note on the kitchen table: *Thank you*.

As he would tell her later, because he paid her a visit once or twice a year, rather than taking revenge on the bald man he roamed the riverside all day long to save the children who had fallen into the water and to teach them to swim. Hoping that they in turn would save other children and would teach them to swim. And when he learned that his mother had compensated the families of the three victims of the Conservatory fire, or that she was going to finance the school's reconstruction, and name its new performance hall after Moli, he said to himself: She's only doing it to win back my love. But even if Moli's mother herself forgave me, I would never be able to forget the evil I did. Then, hoping that his beloved could hear his thoughts, he added that if he no longer dreamt of rejoining her it was just because he'd realized that he could better cleanse himself of his sins by saving lives. And that idea – to devote each of his days to saving lives in order to redeem those he had destroyed – gave him new strength, he said, to combat the demons he'd inherited from his begetter.

41

ARI RETURNED to the barley kingdom eight years after his departure for the capital, when he learned that his grandmother was dying, and his sole and unique desire was to see her again one last time.

"I would have so much wished, before disappearing, to help you recover your joy, but I don't remember what to do," she said when he got to her bedside. "Ah! Old age. I don't even have the strength to apply a bit of rouge to mask my decay. What a disgrace, my God! The picture you'll remember me by!"

"You can go in peace, grandma. For me you will always have the face you had when I listened to your stories while I drank your hot chocolate."

Then, so she would not worry about him, he lied:

"Also, I have a wife who brings me much joy."

"And children?"

"A bunch."

"So that's why you're so poorly dressed. They must cost you a fortune. Take this," she said, slipping her hand into her grandson's pocket. "Don't tell your mother. You'll go to see her, yes?"

He'd intended to pay a visit to the cemetery and then to leave.

"It's the last favour I will ask of you. As much for her as for you. The last gasp of any dying person is for his mama. Don't add to your regrets."

When, after having left the room, he looked in his pocket, he found six gold bracelets. And when he left the house, he came upon the barley queen's chauffeur. Fearing that her eldest would leave without seeing her, she had sent her limousine to take him to the castle. Ari, even if he was certain that his last thought on his deathbed would not be for his mother, told the chauffeur that he would pass by later, then he went to visit Moli's grave and that of his father, to whom he spoke now more frequently than when he was alive. He also wanted to talk to Moli's mother, but she refused to open her door.

It was Junior who greeted him when he arrived at the castle. He too was now a man, and his mother had found him a wife to help him to administer the barley kingdom and to extend the line. As for the queen mother she had aged, but hid it well beneath her makeup, her pant suit, and the perfume that, since his childhood, evoked tender words and kisses.

"My sunlight, my joy," she said, embracing him.

He no longer wanted to avenge anyone, but he could not return a single kiss from his mother, nor pronounce a single word that she wanted to hear.

"When you were little, you made drawings for me, you gathered flowers, promised to take me around the world when you were big. Why have you become so hard, so cold? I am your mother."

How could she behave as if nothing had happened? She certainly had not lost her memory, since she remembered everything that served her interests and could help her to impose her will.

"And as a mother, my heart breaks with sorrow when I hear that the being I love the most in the world," she said with her usual tact in front of Junior, who simply lowered his eyes, "has let a youthful misstep destroy him. Why, my angel? Why do you insist on punishing yourself? Have you learned nothing from your history books? Entire peoples have disappeared. We mourn them for a day or two, we wipe our tears, and we carry on. Life would have no meaning otherwise. If you are determined to insist on redeeming yourself with your swimming lessons, at least do it properly. Build swimming pools. Hire master swimmers. Live up to your name. I'll give you all the money you need. Take it. It's stupid to prevent oneself from being happy."

He knew that she was holding out her hand only to take him under her thumb. Because for her, words served only to grab, contrary to his grandma, who had no need of words to give. But rather than trot out his home truths once again, he bit his tongue and left the barley kingdom two hours later. Furious all the same that his mother once more was able to affect him and to upset him.

"How can you immunize yourself against a parent?" he asked on his next visit to the ER doctor.

"I've spent the day attending to sores and wounds. Can't we talk about something more cheerful?"

He read books on the subject. Like the river waters, the answers that he found whirled for a moment before his eyes, then disappeared. But not the questions. The questions were always there, like the river's banks. The only things that seemed to resist the current, like a branch caught between two rocks, were the small beings just starting their lives who were learning to swim with him. He wasn't sure if they would teach others to swim in turn, if they would even take the trouble to save someone who was drowning. His only certainty was that he had to teach children to swim. As for the rest, it was like clawing at water.

About the Author

Pan Bouyoucas is a Montreal prize-winning novelist, playwright and translator whose novels and plays have been translated into several languages. Two of his novels were written originally in English: *The Man Who Wanted to Drink Up the Sea*, which was selected by France's FNAC as one of the 12 best novels of 2005, and *The Tattoo*, which was longlisted for the 2012 Re-Lit Award. *Ari and the Barley Queen* is the fourth of Pan's French-language novels to be translated into English under the Guernica imprint, the previous three being *A Father's Revenge* (2001), *Portrait of a Husband with the Ashes of His Wife* (2018) and *Cock-A-Doodle-Doo* (2022).

About the Translator

Sheila Fischman studied sciences at the University of Toronto, going on to attempt translating a Quebec novel as a way of improving her knowledge of French. That first novel, *La Guerre, Yes Sir!* by Roch Carrier was a critical and commercial success and her knowledge of French is now much improved. She has translated some 200 novels and collections of short stories, receiving among others the Governor General's award and the Félix-Antoine Savard award. Her authors include Anne Hébert, Marie-Claire Blais, Gaétan Soucy, Louise Desjardins, François Gravel, and Yves Beauchemin. She is a Member of the Order of Canada and a *chevalière* of l'Ordre national du Québec. Sheila Fischman lives in Montreal.